# Lipstick Killah

**Lock Down Publications and Ca$h Presents**
# Lipstick Killah
**A Novel by *Mimi***

Lipstick Killah

# Lock Down Publications

P.O. Box 870494

Mesquite, Tx 75187

Copyright 2018 Lipstick Killah

Printed in the United States of America

*This is a work of fiction. Names, characters, places, and incidents either are products of the author's imagination or are used fictitiously. Any similarity to actual events or locales or persons, living or dead, is entirely coincidental.*

**Lock Down Publications**
**Like our page on Facebook: Lock Down Publications @**
www.facebook.com/lockdownpublications.ldp
Cover design and layout by: **Dynasty Cover Me**
Book interior design by:  **Shawn Walker**
Edited by: Christina Blue

3

Mimi

# Stay Connected with Us!

Text **LOCKDOWN** to 22828 to stay up-to-date with new releases, sneak peaks, contests and more…
Or CLICK HERE to sign up.

Thank you!

## Like our page on Facebook:

**Lock Down Publications:**  Facebook

**Join** Lock Down Publications/The New Era Reading Group

## Follow us on Instagram:

**Lock Down Publications:** Instagram

Email Us: We want to hear from you!

## Submission Guideline.

Submit the first three chapters of your completed manuscript to ldpsubmissions@gmail.com, subject line: Your book's title. The manuscript must be in a .doc file and sent as an attachment. Document should be in Times New Roman, double spaced and in size 12 font. Also, provide your synopsis and full contact information. If sending multiple submissions, they must each be in a separate email.

Have a story but no way to send it electronically? You can still submit to LDP/Ca$h Presents. Send in the first three chapters, written or typed, of your completed manuscript to:

LDP: Submissions Dept
Po Box 870494
Mesquite, Tx 75187

*DO NOT send original manuscript. Must be a duplicate.*

Provide your synopsis and a cover letter containing your full contact information.

Thanks for considering LDP and Ca$h Presents.

# Mimi

# Chapter - One
## Reign

Reign sped through the streets of Brooklyn on her Yoshimura R-55 pink and black motorcycle, trying to get to her next destination. She cursed herself for losing her target due to the fact that some guy was trying to get her attention. One thing she did do was grab his number to deal with him at a later time. Getting caught at a red light, she watched as the candy apple red Bentley Continental GT gained further distance. The occupant had no idea she was getting ready to play the grim reaper. For two weeks, she tailed her victim, getting to know his routine and tonight was the night.

The light turned green and her bike lurched forward, as she tried to play catch up when the Bentley turned a corner two blocks up. As she rounded that same corner, she stopped her bike and planted her feet to the ground, holding her bike steady between her legs. Her target wasn't that far ahead so she took the opportunity to raise her arm and aim. Allowing her Glock to speak for her, she sucked her teeth as she knew none of the bullets hit its target. Revving the engine up, she balanced her bike under her weight and continued on after Kane Speeding further down the block, she noticed the Bentley had parked. A hail of bullets flew around her. Deciding to get off the bike a couple of cars ahead, she reached for her Glock nine that fit snugly inside her boot. She crouched down by a black minivan and fired back. Kane, her victim, clearly had no aim as he fired wildly in the air. Reign was hired to kill Kane by a scorned mother.

Janessa dated Kane for four years, until one day her seventeen-year-old honor roll student turned up pregnant. And Kane was the baby's father. If he didn't die tonight, she was out of twenty thousand dollars.

Wedging her small frame between two cars, she waited for Kane to stop shooting at her. He yelled profusely, and her only hope was for him to shut up. Finally, she heard his footsteps coming her way. Before he could make it to her, she popped up and aimed her gun. She squeezed the trigger lightly, causing the bullet to strike Kane in his chest, dropping him instantly. Her Steve Madden wedge boots padded against the pavement as she made her way towards her target. Reign looked for the gun and noticed that it had slid a safe distance away near a store front with its gate down.

Reign raised her foot and brought it down to his torso, cracking a few ribs in the process.

She said, "That was for shooting at me with your stupid ass."

Kane struggled to cough, as he laughed. "Ahh, man. I must not be doing something right if they sent a bitch after me."

"There is no they. It's only one person and she paid me a hefty amount to make sure that I send you to your maker." Sirens rang in the distance, so she stood over Kane, and pointed her gun between his eyes.

"At least you could tell me who sent you. I'd like to know who to haunt in their sleep."

Tossing the idea around in her head, she bent down and searched his face to see if he was scared. Nothing came across his face except a smirk.

Reign began, "It's a shame that I have to kill you. You are one fine motherfucker. Janessa wishes that you rot in hell."

With that, Reign pulled the trigger sending brain matter all over the side walk and on her shoes. Reaching into her jacket pocket, she pulled out her gold Christian Louboutin lipstick. She admired it for a second, her favorite shade of Very Privy before she opened it and grabbed Kane's wrist, and lifted up his sleeve and drew a heart on it. Satisfied with her job she stood up and got ready to get ghost. Swaying her hips, she made it to her bike and revved the engine, flying down the street as NYPD flew around the corner on two wheels. Reign couldn't help but to laugh as she made her way to her next destination. To collect the remaining balance that was due to her.

\*\*\*

By the time the sun came up, the news of Kane's death spread like wild fire. Every news station was on the story and each one reported that there wasn't a suspect. Reign comfortably slept in her California king sized bed without a care in the world. For Reign, she was born into her lifestyle, if she had to choose to be anything in the world, she would still choose to be a hired assassin. Reign's father, when she was just a little girl, was the best of the best and if there was anyone who had a problem that needed to be erased, they called K.B. As she grew up, K.B taught her the business and everything that he knew. He wanted to make sure that she was set for life and could protect herself, if he was no longer around. Knowing that he was preparing his one and only baby girl for the world, made him proud and he felt like with his guidance and wisdom, she would be able to conquer everything that came her way.

When Reign was only four years old, her mother passed away due to a cancerous tumor that was located on the right side of her brain. Over the years, doctors tried to keep the tumor small, but nothing worked. Both K.B and Angie concluded that death for Angie was near and they had no choice but to accept it. Shortly after Reign's fourth birthday, K.B woke up to get ready for his day. Angie's sickness couldn't stop him from providing for his family, no matter how much he wanted to spend the last days with his wife. As much as he wanted to, Angie always protested that he go out and do what he had to do. He respected her wishes by doing so.

Placing his feet on the ground on his side of the bed, he stretched. He stopped because he knew something wasn't right. Walking over to Angie's side of the bed, tears threatened to fall because she was too peaceful. Placing his hand over her heart, he felt no heartbeat and knew that he lost the love of his life. His tears fell silently as he made a vow to make sure that Reign had the best of everything and to always make sure she knew everything about her mother.

The day of Reign's high school graduation, K.B was talking with his wife, Angie, as he usually did since she passed. The pain he was having in his left arm was one that he was trying to ignore. Reign knocked on his bedroom door to let him know that she was ready. K.B looked at how beautiful his daughter was. Reign stood there dressed in an olive green strapless dressed that puffed out like a tu-tu. Her suede Versace pumps matched her dress perfectly. She wore her mother's diamond stud earrings and diamond and gold necklace. K.B grabbed his suit jacket and they made their way to the stretch limo he'd rented just for her. Reign was an only child and when it came to expenses, he went all out to make sure that she wanted for nothing.

Once they arrived at the high school, the graduation began. With each minute that passed, the pain K.B felt got intense. He prayed that whatever was causing him pain, would allow him to see his one and only baby girl cross the stage. Soon enough they began to call each student names. It seemed like it took forever to reach the M's. At least that's how it felt to K.B.

"Reign Mills," the principal finally called. K.B jumped up and like any proud parent would, he hollered like his life depended on it. Reign turned with a smile on her face towards her dad. She knew something was wrong as everything slowed down around her. K.B.'s face expressed hurt, as his hand shot to his chest.

"Call 911!" Reign shouted and came out of her shoes to rush to her father's side. Reign was too late. K.B was gone by the time they made it to the hospital. Reign had been a ticking time bomb since then.

\*\*\*

The sun was just going down when Reign decided to roll out of bed. Reaching over to her night stand, she grabbed the blunt that she had left in the ashtray and lit it up. After a few pulls she put it out and grabbed her phone heading to the bathroom. Messages from her best friend were plentiful from the night before, of course cursing her out for not going out with her. She finished up in the bathroom and went back to enjoy her blunt. Just as she got comfortable, her best friend called her.

"What's up, trick?" Reign asked, picking up the phone.

"Bitch, you missed the most epic night ever!" Pearl shouted into the phone.

"First of all, don't yell in my ear. It's too early for your shit. Every time you go out you have an epic time."

Pearl paused before she answered. She said, "While that may be true, last night took the cake."

"How so, Pearl?" Reign feigned interest. She knew where this story was going and knew it was going to be the same shit.

"Okay, so you remember how I told you about that millionaire record exec that I met?"

"Yes, I'm listening?"

"We got a little cozy last night and I rapped for him. He invited me down to his office on Monday to pick up a contract. Would you like to come with me? Just to make sure everything is on the up and up?" Pearl asked excitedly.

Reign was super excited for Pearl. She couldn't help but to agree to go with her.

Reign said, "I'll go. But you have to promise me that when you become a millionaire, you're going to buy me the biggest house that you ever did see."

With laughter, Pearl said, "I got you. What are you doing? I feel like going out and catching me somebody husband or baby father."

"Girl, you know that I'm not even on that type of time. I really don't understand how you could do that."

"Girl, I'm just tired of these niggas. They can't be loyal for shit but expect for you to do their laundry, give them a home cooked meal, and sex them every thirteen and a half minutes. You give them all of that and they still manage to cheat. I swear I'd rather be some nigga side bitch. Less hassle and you ain't gotta worry about wifey duties. Just fuck them and send them home."

"So, you think it's okay to be fucking another bitches man. That's so trifling," Reign replied with disgust.

"I'd rather swallow his kids then to be birthing them. And that's a fact, baby doll."

"You irk every fiber of my soul. I'm going to be picking you up in an hour," Reign replied with laughter.

"You got it." With that, Reign hung up and decided that she'd finish her blunt while searching for an outfit to wear.

Looking in her closet, Reign thought to herself, '*I really need to go shopping. All this black.*' Shaking her head, she picked up a light grey V-neck short sleeved shirt, black skinny leg Guess jeans and her black open toed chunky heels. Reign moved on to her bathroom which was her little slice of heaven in her home. Decorated in pink and white, her favorite colors, despite her taste in apparel. She felt an overwhelming comfort wash over her every time she entered. After she made sure the water was to her liking, she disrobed, watching herself in the mirror. Her milk chocolate skin laid flawlessly over her bone structure with barely any blemish or scar. Of course, in her line of work, she'd get a few bumps and bruises but none that ever lasted three days.

Reign stood at five feet ten inches, inheriting her height from her father. Her pear-shaped body came from her mother from what she saw in the pictures that her father used to show her. Her breasts were just the right size at a 34C. Her waist was small, but her ass and hips blossomed out, hence her pear shape. Her eyes were a deep shade of brown and when the light hit them just right you could see speckles of green in them. Her natural hair was always a thick Afro with tiny ringlets of curls. Reign always had the option of straightening her hair, but she'd rather braid it up in a protective style and always rocked twenty-four-inch virgin Brazilian hair.

After her shower, she moisturized her skin with organic coconut oil and got dressed. It was very rare for Reign to socialize, but she'd figured what harm would it be to just go out and have one drink with Pearl. Reign was dressed in ten minutes flat and on her way out of the door. She sent Pearl a message as she climbed into her Audi A-4.

# Mimi

# Chapter – Two
## Senaj

For the longest, all Senaj wanted to do was help children. Being of African descent, Senaj; although he had never been to Africa, knew the struggles that children from his homeland faced. Senaj was born and raised in the United States, Brooklyn, New York to be exact. His parents were from the Republic of Congo; one of the poorest countries in Africa. They moved to the United States years before Senaj was born, when they only had his older brother Akuchi.

As a child, Senaj saw how hard his parents struggled and vowed that once he made it in his profession, he'd take care of them. That was until he went off to college and sustained a job, and his parents moved to Florida to retire. Leaving himself and Akuchi in New York. Only for Senaj to be left out in the real world on his own because his only brother was sent to do a fifteen-year bid for attempted murder. Outside of his residency and as much as he could, Senaj volunteered at Ridgewood Bushwick Youth Center in Brooklyn.

For Senaj, it seemed like it had been forever since he has been out to enjoy himself. He had always been busy with his studies and residency since he started three years ago in 2013. He had six months left to complete before he was to get his certification to become a pediatrician. This night was the first night he had off for a week and Senaj, his two best friends, Rasheed and Polite, decided to head out to Smalls Jazz Club in Greenwich Village. Senaj was never the type to be seen inside of a club but if he chose to go to one, he chose to hit a laid back underground one.

He pulled up to Smalls Jazz Club and looked at himself in the rear-view mirror to make sure he had nothing on his face. He was a very handsome man with skin the color of

15

vanilla beans. He may have been darker than most but was fine nonetheless. Light brown eyes, a button nose and medium full lips adorned his face. When he smiled, he showed all his white teeth, that were almost perfect. Excluding the chipped tooth on the left side that he refused to get fixed. Only because it was a reminder of his brother. When they were younger they fought quite often, but one time, Akuchi was furious that Senaj had touched his clothing and head butted Senaj, causing him to see stars.

Now at age twenty-seven, Senaj towered over most, at six feet six inches. Working out was a part of his life style and he made sure that he was muscular, just right for his height. His body was his temple and he treated it as such for the most part. He would only drink on occasion, he never smoked, and ate somewhat healthy.

"Ahh, man. Look at this fool always checking himself out." Senaj heard his friend Polite say.

Turning to his right, he saw his friends watching him through the window. He could do nothing except laugh and climb his tall frame out of his Honda Civic. He gave each one of them dap and leaned against the car.

"How long y'all been here?" he asked, rubbing his hand over the stubble that was on his chin.

"We just got here. It looks like it may be a full house already with all these damn cars out here," Rasheed noted.

"Only on the day that I decide to come out would it be packed. It's a Tuesday, you would think that people would be home," Senaj said.

Polite jumped in and said, "You would think, but look at us. We have to go to work in the morning and we're here."

Senaj laughed and said, "Y'all got to work, not me. Let's go inside. I'm in need of a beer."

All together they walked in and found empty seats in a far corner. Rasheed walked up to the bar and ordered them a round of beers and took his seat. Senaj had been friends with Rasheed and Polite since Junior High School. Polite whose real name was Braxton, was a bully back then and would always bother Senaj calling him an "African booty scratcher" and other things of that nature. Senaj, who was already friends with Rasheed at the time, got tired of Polite calling him names and beat him up. Two weeks after the fight, Polite figured since he started the fight, he could be the bigger person and apologize. Since then, they been tight.

As the fellas caught up, two beautiful women walked in, grabbing their attention. Senaj couldn't take his eyes off the taller one and he instantly thought about climbing all over her tall frame, even if he was taller. He drooled as he watched her as her head fell back in laughter as she took a seat with the other female she was with.

Polite interrupted Senaj's gaze by saying, "So, I guess what we're talking about isn't good enough."

Rasheed broke out into laughter momentarily causing the two women to look in their direction. The shorter of the two gave a polite smile, while the taller one sent a look their way that sent chills down their spines.

Senaj said, "I can't help myself. She's beautiful."

"I can't front they both are. And you know what's crazy, they both have on a decent amount of clothing. The way females dress now, it's hard to not hope to see a titty pop out," Rasheed spoke.

"You not lying about that. Me personally, I don't mind hoping to see a titty pop out," Polite said, with a smile on his face.

Senaj shook his feeling away and focused back on his friends. For the most part of two hours, they talked shit and caught up with each other while stealing glances at the beautiful women who appeared to have forgotten that they were even there. Until Senaj, who had one too many beers, decided to go over to the women to say hi and offer them a drink.

17

# Mimi

"Good evening ladies. How are you doing?" he asked, reaching their table.

Their laughter ceased as they looked up at him. Senaj was looking at the taller girl, while the shorter one eyed him. Polite and Rasheed had walked over to the bar to get a better view at their friend getting rejected.

"Hello. We're doing just fine," the short one responded.

"Can I offer you ladies a drink?" His attention still on the tall girl, who busied herself on her phone.

"No, we're good." The tall one finally spoke.

"Ahh, and she speaks," Senaj responded, sarcastically.

With a roll of her eyes, she looked up at him and something sparked inside of her, but she ignored it. She said, "Oh, I speak. Just not to you. Now if you're done, you could go back to your boys."

"Reign!" The short girl sounded exasperated.

Senaj smirked, as he walked away now knowing her name. He stored it in his memory bank, just in case he ran into her again. From the distance he could see that the two were now in a heated exchange, but he was satisfied. For the rest of the night, Senaj enjoyed himself with his friends.

\*\*\*

Two days later, Senaj decided to do a little bit of shopping for some more suits, so he headed to Downtown Brooklyn. As he walked out of Foot Locker, he paused as he saw the girl from the jazz club. She was at a light and she took her helmet off and shook her hair free. He knew he couldn't pass up this second chance, he just knew it was fate that he was seeing her again. Before the light could change, he made his way towards her with a smile on his face. He stood right in front of her motorcycle causing her to place her hand towards her boot until she recognized his face.

"You want to move or get hit?" she spoke.

18

"As long as I get your number in the process it doesn't matter to me," he spoke, unbeknownst to him, his voice caused shivers down her spine.

"What if I hit you and you still don't get my number?"

"You wouldn't. At least not in broad daylight."

"I've done worse in broad daylight."

Senaj cracked a smile and cars behind them honked their horns. He said, "All you have to do is give me your number and I'll be out of your way."

"You don't quit, do you?" Reign said.

"No, and I don't care if I am holding up traffic. Once I set my eyes on something I go for it."

Reign looked at him up and down as she contemplated giving him her number. Cars sped around them and cursed them out. By the time the light turned red again for the second time, she decided that she would take his number instead.

She smirked and said, "Happy? I have your number."

"That's the easy part. You would actually have to call me. I'll be going back to do my residency soon, so I hope you call sooner rather than later."

"Residency? You're a doctor?" she asked, with wide eyes.

With a wink, Senaj said, "We'll talk about that when you call."

The light turned green again and as smoothly as he could, he walked away and made it to the parking garage to pick up his car. He was a happy camper.

# Mimi

## Chapter -Three
## Reign

Reign went the whole day thinking about the guy who stopped her in the middle of the street. It had been so long since a guy showed interest in her that it made her scared. She had such an intimidating persona, that it had been six years since she last spoke to a guy. Let alone take somebody number. Reign's last relationship didn't end so well. She tried her luck by falling in love and letting all her guards down.

For three years, she ignored the signs of his infidelity. Left and right, chicks were saying they were sleeping with Josiah. She found text messages and panties in her laundry that she knew for a fact that they didn't belong to her. Still in all, she chose to ignore the signs because she was deeply in love with him. That was until she walked in their home and knew that something was off. Josiah usually would be out all day and if he had to stop by the house, he'd let her know and when she walked in, she was surprised that his .380 was sitting on the coffee table. Grabbing the gun, she made her way upstairs and climbed them cautiously. Stepping over the one that made a noise if it was stepped on. Before she knew it, the tears were running down her face. The sounds of the head board banging against the wall played just as much in her head as it did in the room.

As she got closer to the bedroom door, she heard Josiah's familiar grunts of satisfaction. The door was already cracked open, so she nudged the door open with the butt of the gun and aimed it at the bitch with the fake titties and sent a bullet straight to her dome. Instantly she fell in a heap on top of Josiah. Shocked, Josiah pushed the girl from off top of him and rolled out of the bed, using the sheet to cover his body.

Hitting the light switch, the lights flickered before they

turned completely on. Reign sniffled and said, "You have the audacity to cover your body after you've been caught fucking another bitch in our bed!"

Josiah stared at Reign wide eyed as he studied the gun in her hand. He said, "Listen, baby..."

"And your dick is still hard! You know what, I've stuck by your side time and time again when people would tell me that you were cheating. I played dumb seeing text message after text message with girls asking when you were gonna fuck them. Even sending you pictures of your nut in their mouths and all types of nasty shit. And here I am still fucking with your damn ass."

"Reign, let me explain please!" Josiah pleaded.

"I gave you the money to put you on, stuck by your side when you didn't have two nickels to rub together in your dirty ass hands, Washed your funky ass holey ass, shitty ass drawers! And this is what you do!" The tears had stopped, and the hurt was gone. She was filled with rage and all she saw was blood.

"Babe. This was a simple mistake that we could get through."

Sucking her teeth, she said, "One time would be a mistake but once you do it consistently, it becomes a decision. Fuck you, nigga!"

Without a further thought, Reign shot him multiple times until he fell over next to the chick she caught him with. Sitting down on her bed, her eyes were dripping wetness. This was the first time she had felt remorse for killing. She had been in love with Josiah and gave him her all. She saw the Christian Louboutin lipstick he had given her as a gift. She drew a heart on his wrist symbolizing the love she had for him. She drew an X on the thing that he had cheated on her with. Catching herself from throwing up, she rushed out of the room and called her clean-up crew. This was the last time she had used the clean-up crew

Lipstick Killah

because they had done such a lousy job and the police found
their bodies. That was when she started getting called the
Lipstick Killah. Shaking that memory from her mind, she
heard her phone ringing. She pulled it out recognizing the
number.

"Hello." she spoke.

"Hey there, baby girl."

A smile spread across her face as she said, "Hi, Uncle
James. How are you?"

"I'm hanging in there, baby girl." There was a pause
before he continued, and Reign knew that it couldn't be
good.

Slowly, Uncle James began talking again, "Listen, baby
girl, I need you to come on over to the house. There is
something I need to discuss with you."

"Okay. How soon you need me there?" she asked. Her
heart pounded in her chest.

"Yesterday." Without anything else being said, Uncle
James hung up.

Reign jumped out of her chair she sat in at the kitchen
table and placed her sneakers on her feet. Grabbing her keys,
purse, Glock, and some money, she flew out of the door and
to the buildings garage. She wasted no time to get to Park
Slope where Uncle James had retired too. Uncle James was
deep in the game as her father was and not only was he a
hired killer, he sold drugs of any sort and if he had to, he
would have sold purses just because. He was addicted to
money.

Reign made it to Uncle James house in record time and
rushed inside. She didn't have to find him because he was
sitting in the living room. Reign figured the reason he called
her over was because he was falling ill but from what she
could see, he was fine. She leaned in to give him a hug and
sat down next to him.

"What's up, Uncle James? I thought you were going to

tell me that you were sick," Reign spoke.

Uncle James smiled and said, "I may be old, but I'm as healthy as an ox."

"So, what's up?"

"That dude Kane that you killed a couple of days ago, he has some powerful friends."

"So?"

"What do you mean so? They are looking for his killer and they aren't the type to not find out."

"Uncle James, if they do we'll go toe to toe. I'm not worried about it."

"Reign, I need for you to take this serious. Kane was a part of this small but powerful group of people called the Asesino Cartel. That's Spanish for killer. They are an elite group of killers and dope pushers and when one of their people are killed, they hunt until they find who did it. When they do, they torture them for days until they get tired of it and kill them."

"Uncle James, have you forgotten that I was trained by the best? Your brother, I can handle myself."

Uncle James sighed exasperatedly and looked at Reign. He didn't want to have to tell her what he was about to tell her, but she needed to know.

He began, "Your father, God bless his soul, was a hot head. While he did handle his business, he also pissed a lot of people off. One of those was this dude named Perry. He was a part of this cartel and your father had been sleeping with his wife. This was before your mother. K.B was a bold motherfucker, flaunting Perry's wife around without a care in the world and he knew whose wife she was, he just didn't give a fuck. One day, Perry had gotten enough, and he decided to follow your father and his wife around just to get a feel of what they were doing. That was until they went back to his house and fucked for hours. That man sat outside of his own home while they did so. The sun had

24

gone down an hour before Perry decided to get out of the car. He crept inside and caught your father while he was taking a piss, butt ass naked. His wife begged and pleaded for Perry to leave K.B alone, that she was the one who he was angry with. That woman must have loved your father more than Perry because she begged him to kill her instead of your father.

"Anyway, her pleading fell on deaf ears, because he dragged your father out of his house and threw him in the trunk of his car. Your father told me he didn't recognize where he was when they had finally stopped. Perry grabbed your father by the neck and they walked into this warehouse. K.B. said they had to have been somewhere upstate because he was surrounded by woods."

Reign was so engrossed in the story. She had never heard this one and she and her father used to stay up all night while he told her about his past.

"Uncle James, you can't just leave off there. Obviously, Daddy got away, and I want to know how," Reign said, pouting like a little girl.

Uncle James chuckled and said, "Your father has never told you this story?"

"Obviously not, Uncle James. You got me on the edge of my seat. Part of me is listening because it's suspenseful but the other side of me is wanting to know what happens just in case I run into those people."

Although he knew he had Reign's undivided attention, he decided to prolong the story by going into the kitchen to pour himself a drink. Reign leaned back onto the couch waiting for Uncle James to return. Winding her thumbs around each other, she hated the fact Uncle James was doing this purposely. A few minutes later, Uncle James walked inside of the living room with a smirk on his face.

"Your father must have been locked inside of this warehouse for three days. After Perry dropped him off, no one came. He didn't eat anything, he didn't drink anything, so on that third day when Perry came back, he figured that your father would be weak and wouldn't put up a fight. Perry underestimated him because your father handed him an ass whopping of a life time. K.B. knew mixed martial arts and he had a lot of discipline. When he told me this story, he told me when Perry found him, he was still naked, of course but he was playing possum. Laid out." Uncle James paused while he laughed and sipped his drink.

"K.B. said that he allowed Perry to get close to him before he snatched his foot from under him, snapping it in the process. Perry fell to the ground and tried to grab his gun from his waist, but your father was fast. He knocked the gun from his hands and delivered blow after blow onto Perry's body. Your father could have easily picked up the gun and shot him, but he was so upset that he waited until he was inches away from death to snap his neck."

Reign interrupted and said, "All he had to do was snap his neck?"

"Baby girl, that is not the end. He stole Perry's clothes and left the warehouse with the gun. He didn't know that he had a whole team of motherfuckers surrounding the warehouse. All he had was a six shooter. For a moment he fooled them because he had on Perry's clothes. When they noticed that instead of him going back towards them, he went towards the woods. They opened fire on him as he took flight only occasionally shooting back. As he got a safe distance away and out of bullets he ran in the darkness until he ended up at an old woman's house. It was months before anyone saw him and for sure word began to spread that your father was killed. But I knew he wasn't. He's my brother and I knew in my heart that he wasn't dead. As winter approached that's when K.B. began to show his face and we teamed up with our best men and took down more than half of them. They eventually called a truce due to all the bloodshed. Once myself and your father got our crew together, we were a force to be reckoned with. They didn't want that type of static. From that point on we stayed out of each other's way."

Reign exhaled as she took it all in. K.B. was a super hero to her and in a strange way it warmed her heart to hear this story about her father. Reign said with a chuckle, "My dad was the shit."

Uncle James got serious and said, "Baby girl, I told you that story because once these motherfuckers find out that K.B.'s daughter killed one of their own, they are going to start an all-out war. And I will be forced out of retirement. Not that it would be an issue, but all of this could have been prevented, if you would have come to me first. You know that this is how it works. For you to get your cases from me. We go through them together and you go do what you have to do. I don't know what you thought you were doing when you decided to go to that woman and take an order from her."

"Uncle James, she was distraught in a McDonald's. I couldn't help but want to help her," Reign explained.

She knew her uncle was pissed because she knew how it worked. Reign was to never randomly pick up a job without it going through him first. It was his way of making sure that she stayed safe.

Slamming his glass against the coffee table, he shouted, "Reign, you know the rules! I wouldn't give a flying fuck if the bitch was laying in her own vomit covered in blood! Or inches away from death!"

"Uncle James-"

"Uncle James, my ass! You know you need to stay out of the streets for a while. However, I will give you this last case. It's a one point five-million-dollar contract. I'll take five hundred thousand and you put the rest away. At least for six months. But you have to complete this first."

Reign looked at Uncle James like he had another head growing from his neck. *'How can he ask me to take one last case right after he tells me that I need to stay out of the streets?'* She thought to herself.

"What if I decline? I mean you did just tell me to stay out of the streets," Reign spoke. She knew that she wasn't going to decline because of the amount of money that she would gain. She would be crazy if she would turn that down. By all means, she doesn't need it only because her account and her "rainy day" money was sitting proper.

"If you decline, then you decline. I won't force you to do it. If I know my niece the way I know her, she's not going to give this case up."

Reign narrowed her eyes into slits because he did know her. She chuckled on the inside and told him she would begin in a few days. With a hug and a kiss on the cheek, she left her uncle's house with her thoughts swimming. She'd been in this game since she was twenty. Now at twenty-six, how could she stop? What would she do while on this hiatus? Even more so, where would she go? These were the questions that she would figure out in the next couple of days before she began her last case.

***

Once Reign left Uncle James house, he received a phone call that turned his stomach into knots. The relationship between Reign and Uncle James from Reign's point of view was peachy keen. On the other hand, while he loved Reign, he despised the fact that his brother left her everything. But he knew that someone knew and would eventually tell Reign. Uncle James planned to find out and gather everything K.B left Reign.

"James, I don't know how much longer you expect me to wait. Your deadline was two weeks ago," The person on the other end spoke.

In a hushed tone, Uncle James said, "I know. I just need more time."

The other end was silent for a few moments and then the person said, "I don't give out extensions often, but I like you, kid. You have one more week and if not, everything that you worked so hard for to keep a secret will come crashing down."

"I understand." With that the phone went silent and three beeps rang in James' ear indicating that the call ended.

James knew that he was in a fucked-up predicament and knew that if he didn't deliver then his life would be on the line or his niece's. And with the way that he was feeling he wouldn't mind it being his niece.

# Mimi

# Chapter - Four
## Senaj

The time for Senaj to go back to doing his residency was dwindling down. He had two days left, and it was stressing him out, waiting for Reign to call him. She had been on his mind since she took his number down, a day and a half ago. Senaj felt it in his gut that she was out of his league, but he couldn't help but want to get to know this woman.

Senaj was enjoying his morning, laying under his comforter in his air-conditioned room, when his phone started vibrating on his night stand. The news had reported that the day was going to be humid with a thirty percent chance of rain and if that was either one of his friends wanting to go out, he would have to decline. Fortunately, it wasn't Polite nor Rasheed. It was an unknown number.

"Hello," Senaj answered.

"May I speak with Senaj Ademyemi, please?" A polite soft voice came through the phone. Almost childlike.

"Speaking. May I ask who is calling?" he asked sitting up in his bed. He figured that it could have been one of the kids from the youth center in need of help. There was silence on the other and as he prepared to ask who it was again, she spoke up.

"It's Reign," she said.

Senaj couldn't help the smile that spread across his face.

"Hey, how are you?" he asked.

"I'm well and yourself? Are you busy?" Reign asked, getting straight to the point.

"No, I'm not. I'm actually just waking up."

"Did I wake you?" Reign asked, innocently.

"No, not all." There was silence on both ends of the phone for a few moments. Both wondering what to say next. She finally spoke.

"Would you like to meet me at Central Park?"

"Yes, sure. Just give me an hour to get ready and I'll head on over."

A smile crept onto Reign's face and she said, "Okay. See you then."

Three beeps indicated that the phone call was disconnected, Senaj looked at the phone screen to make sure that it actually hung up and jumped out of the bed. He did a little happy dance that kind of resembled the Milly Rock, stiffening his body and swinging his arms in tight circles close to his body. He knew he was doing it right but the excitement he couldn't contain overshadowed his ability to dance. He walked into his closet and found some blue jean shorts, a white graphic tee, and his black and white shell top Adidas. After his outfit was set he jumped into the shower. He couldn't contain his excitement as he thought about going to meet up with Reign.

Once done with his shower, he moisturized his body and got dressed. As he grabbed his keys, his phone rang in his pocket. Looking at the display he knew by the unknown number, it was his brother calling him from prison.

"Hello," he answered. The automatic operator instructed for him to press three to accept the call and he did so.

"Hello," his brother said through the receiver once the call was connected.

"Chi! What's up?" Senaj spoke.

"What's going on?"

"Nothing much. How are you doing?"

"I'm well. Can't complain too much with my current situation." Akuchi spoke with a thick African accent. Even though he had been living in America for several years.

"Yeah, I know. You'll be out soon so you won't have much to worry about."

Chi laughed and said, "Brother, five years isn't soon. How are mom and dad?"

# Lipstick Killah

"Living it up in Florida. They think that they're grown."

"You know what to do when you speak with them. But where are you on your way to? I can hear the wind," Chi said, with a chuckle.

"Oh. I met this girl. Man, she is the epitome of beautiful."

"Just because she's beautiful doesn't mean that she's good. You don't need any distractions from your studying."

"I don't even think that she's like that. Well at least from what I gathered the first two times we crossed paths. Today, is our first time actually hanging out."

"You won't truly know until you've known her for some time. I just want you to be careful. That last girl you were with was a bad seed."

"We going to go through this shit, Chi! I'm not with her ass anymore!"

"I have to keep reminding you so that you don't fall for the same shit again."

Senaj sighed because every time he told his brother about a girl that he talked to, Chi would bring up his nothing ass ex, Christina. He hated talking about her because their break up was horrible.

Akuchi spoke but Senaj's mind drifted to his relationship with Christina. When he met her, he had just started college and she caught his eye. He had been skeptical about approaching her because she was so beautiful. He did so anyway, and they ended up becoming inseparable. Seven months into the relationship, Senaj noticed her changing. She'd start an argument for absolutely no reason and quite a few times, she got physical. It would take everything in Senaj to not hit her back. He didn't believe in hitting woman and it didn't matter to him how many times or how hard she'd hit him, he never touched her.

Christina's personality was what won Senaj over but

33

that all dwindled when she changed. Slowly, he withdrew himself from school only to worry about his relationship with Christina. He was sick in love with her. Two months after her change, he began noticing things missing from his dorm room. He didn't have a roommate and he knew that he wasn't misplacing his things. What took the cake for him was when he came home from Christmas break. His game system and TV were missing. Initially, he thought that someone had broken into his room, but his door hadn't been tampered with. Although it wasn't allowed, the only other person who had the key was Christina. He quickly sent her a text letting her know that he was back and to come by as soon as possible.

It took Christina two hours to come to his dorm and when she did, something was off about her. Her eyes were bugged out and her appearance was unkempt. He questioned her about his missing items and she wouldn't give him a straight answer. After an hour of going back and forth, Christina confessed that she had developed a cocaine habit and that she had been cheating on him with a dude that had the same habit. In fact, he was the one who introduced her to it. She broke down and cried, making the biggest scene ever. Senaj was too through and kicked her out. He fell into depression. It affected his education and he almost lost his scholarship. Thanks to his big brother, who tore his ass apart and before anything drastic happened, he was able to get back on track.

"Senaj, did you hear me?" Chi spoke, into the phone.

"Sorry, bro, I didn't hear you. I was thinking about something."

"In short, I told you to be careful with this girl. Keep your head focused. The call is going to end soon so tell mom and dad that I said hi and that I love them."

"You got it, brother."

"I love you, too. And I know I don't say it enough, but

I'm proud of you."

"Thanks, bro. I appreciate it and I love you, too. Hold your head," Senaj managed to say before the call was disconnected. Thinking about Christina put him in a bad mood and he wanted to take a rain check, but he remembered that he still didn't have Reign's number. Senaj decided that he'd still go and try to make the best of things. He put some music on and before he knew it he was pulling up to Central Park. Once he found parking, he exhaled and got out of his car. He never asked where in Central Park she wanted to meet him, so he began to slowly walk towards the fountain. He had been walking for a good ten minutes when his phone rung. Yet again, another unknown number and this time without hesitation, he answered.

"Hello."

"You look nice today." Her voice seeped through the phone.

He paused and looked around but didn't see her.

"Where are you?" he asked.

"Hang up," she instructed.

As she did so, he turned back towards the direction he was walking and noticed her walking in his direction. His breath caught in his throat as he gawked at her. She was wearing light blue mid–thigh length brown shoe boots that laced up in the front, and a white tank top that had *Boss* written across her chest. Her cocoa brown skin glistened under the sun light. Her hair was slicked back into a high ponytail that flowed down to her lower back.

As they grew closer to one another, she looked up at Senaj and for the first time ever, since meeting her, he saw her smile. For him, it was contagious because without realizing it, he smiled back.

"You talking about me looking nice, look at you. Definitely a difference from the last run-in's that I had with you," Senaj said.

Reign slowly spun in a circle making sure she teased him with her assets. "This was just something that I put together at the last minute."

"I'm glad that you did. Shall we?" Senaj said, extending his arm out so that she could grab onto it.

With a smile, she wrapped her arm around his and they began to walk toward the fountain. They enjoyed their walk together without speaking until they got to the fountain.

"So, you're studying to become a doctor?" Reign asked, as they took a seat.

"That I am."

"What kind?"

"A pediatrician."

"Mmm. You must like working with kids?" she asked.

Senaj paused before he answered. Tilting his head for a better look, his eyes squinted against the sun shining in them. He licked his lips, LL Cool J like, before he answered. "Yes. I love working with kids. Whenever I have time off from school, I usually spend my time with the youth at a youth center in Bushwick."

Reign cocked her head and asked, "Do you have any kids?"

Senaj chuckled because he was often asked this question from women that he met because he loved working with kids. "No, I don't have kids. Do you?"

"No."

For the better part of two hours they talked and laughed, getting to know each other better. That was until Reign's phone began to constantly ring. She tried to ignore it but once the person called for the fifth time, she excused herself and took the call. Once she got back to Senaj, she told him that she had to go.

Promising that they would get together again soon, Senaj nodded his head and leaned in for a hug before they headed their separate ways. Deep in his gut he felt like their next meeting wouldn't happen any time soon.

Mimi

## Chapter - Five
## Reign

Reign hated the fact that she had to depart from Senaj. She was just starting to enjoy herself, which was something that she rarely did. Uncle James knew how to fuck up a wet dream. Aggravation set in as Reign made her way back to Brooklyn to meet her uncle. *'Ain't shit about to be important once I meet him.'* Reign thought to herself. She allowed her thoughts wander to the little bit of time that she spent with Senaj and it brought a smile to her face. She learned that his parents and older brother lived in Africa for the most part of their lives and his dream was to at least go and visit The Motherland before he got too old.

Before Reign knew it, she was pulling up to Pier 41 in the heart of Red Hook, located in the southern part of Brooklyn. Reign didn't want to have to deal with Uncle James, but business was just that. Business. She noticed that her uncle was seated on the boardwalk and took a deep breath before exiting her car. Her heels click-clacked as they met the pavement with each step that she took.

"What's up, Uncle James?" she asked, standing in front of him.

Uncle James looked over the water as if he was in deep thought before he decided to open his mouth.

"I need a huge favor from you. It's something that I wouldn't normally ask you to do but you are the only one that I could trust."

Reign raised her eyebrows as she studied his face. She finally spoke up, "And what might that be?"

"My usual runner got caught in a jam and got her ass arrested behind something her baby father did. I need you to make this run for me," Uncle James admitted.

"Uncle James, drugs aren't my thing and you know that. My hands don't get dirty like that," Reign said, copping a

39

slight attitude. Yes, her hands got dirty nonetheless because her murder game was official. She could hide evidence of her killing someone. She had been in the game for quite some time, so she knew the in's and out's. Drugs she knew nothing of and to be quite honest her biggest fear was to be driving down somebody's highway and the cops pulled her over and the trunk is full of drugs. That was a no for her.

"I know, baby girl, but you the only one that I could trust. Believe me, if I had another choice I wouldn't have even asked you. I'll cut you ten percent of the money that you are going to grab."

"Ten percent of how much? How long do I have to think about this? I don't know what my answer is going to be, I have other things on my plate."

"What other things?" he asked.

"Did you forget that you set me up with that million and half contract?" Reign asked, with her arms folded across her chest.

Uncle James pulled at his chin hair looking lost deep in thought. He finally spoke and said, "Nah. I didn't forget. Look, can you let me know by tomorrow? I really need this shit done."

"If it's so important that it gets done, why not do it yourself?"

James looked at Reign like why would she ask such a question. In her mind it only made perfect sense for him to do it. If you need a job done, it's always better for you to do it yourself 'cause you know that shit would go right. Even though her account was sitting proper, that ten percent that he was offering wouldn't hurt. She knew since her uncle was quite known in the game that the money that she would be picking up wouldn't be any chump change.

"You and I both know that, that can't happen," Uncle James finally responded.

"Okay. I'll let you know tomorrow," Reign said.

She hugged her uncle and made her way back to her car. She was unpleasantly put off that she had to stop what she was doing. That was the one thing that she hated about doing what she did. She knew that at any given moment she would have to drop what she was doing to meet with her uncle.

Once Reign got to her car, she called up her best friend, Pearl. They quickly made plans to meet up to grab a bite to eat. Reign's better judgment told her to take her ass home, but she was in desperate need of girl time.

"Hello," Pearl sang into the phone.

"What are you doing?" Reign spoke, connecting her phone to the blue tooth.

"I was just on the phone with Bryson."

"Your lawyer?"

"Yep."

"For what?"

"We were going over the contract that I had gotten from Bobby and there were quite a few things in the contract that Bryson wasn't feeling. He advised me to cut off any sexual communication that I have with him."

"As you shouldn't have even did so to begin with," Reign interrupted.

"Reign, don't start your shit."

"Pearl, you know anything I tell you is only to make sure you're good. I've told you from the beginning that you need to not mix business with pleasure."

"Reign, I'm grown, and I know what I'm doing," Pearl said.

Reign decided to let the subject be because she knew that Pearl was catching an attitude. Pearl hated to be told what to do or told something that would keep her out of harm's way. She was grown and didn't live by anyone's rules except her own.

"You right. You want to meet up at the diner we like to

go to on Second Ave in Midtown?" Reign said, dropping the subject.

"Morning star? Hell yeah, I could go for their French toast sundae. I haven't gotten my advance yet, but I'll treat."

"Girl, you don't have to worry about it. You know I got it."

"Reign, you always pay. Let me pay. Stanley gave me a few dollars."

Reign frowned up her face. She had a certain distaste for Pearl's boyfriend, Stanley. There was something about him that she couldn't put her finger on. She vowed that she would keep her mouth shut until she figured it out.

"Aight, girl. I'll see you there. I'm on my way."

"I'll beat you there. I'm in the area."

They said their goodbyes and hung up. Reign turned her music up as she made her way to the diner. Often times, Pearl worked her nerves something bad, but she wouldn't trade her best friend for anything in this world. They've been hanging tight for more than fifteen years. They got into their first fights together, had their first boyfriends together, and they even got their pussies broke wide open together. When she felt all alone in the world, it was Pearl and her family that took her in and made her feel like family. That was before Uncle James came home and turned her world upside down.

At the thought of Uncle James, she could only let out a huge sigh. She knew something was fishy about him lately. She promised herself that when she had the time, she would figure it out. Quickly putting her Uncle James to the back of her mind, she smiled when Senaj evaded her thoughts. She loved that they connected and the fact that he wasn't some thug. He had goals and wanted to be someone who could actually make a difference. She wondered if her line of business would be too much for him, given if he ever found out. *'Who am I fooling? He's going to be a doctor and if he ever found out what I did to make money, he would run for the hills.* 'She thought to herself.

"My name is Dr. Senaj and this is my girlfriend, Reign. She's a real-life assassin." Reign spoke out loud, causing herself to break out into a fit of giggles. She was reading too much into it and she knew that by all means she would have to hide that aspect of her life away from him.

Twenty minutes later she pulled up to Morning Star Cafe and parked her car. Before getting out of the car, she noticed that the manila envelope that Uncle James gave her was sitting on her passenger seat. Without a thought, she picked it up and the first thing that she noticed was that her next target was fine as hell. She looked at the file and saw that he was married with no kids and he owed a lot of money to the Mexican cartel. She wondered how much he owed for them to put a one point five-million-dollar contract on his head. Pictures of the cars that him and his wife drove were in the file too. Reign was so engrossed in the file that she didn't notice Pearl was standing next to her car. When Reign did notice, Pearl had knocked and scared Reign's heart into her ass. Reign rolled her window down preparing to curse Pearl out.

"Bitch!" Reign began.

"Hell nah, bitch my ass. I've watched you sit in this damn car for fifteen minutes. Get the fuck out before we lose our booth," Pearl spoke.

All Reign could do was put the file under her seat and get out.

"You didn't order yet, right?" she asked.

"I was going to, but I noticed that you were deep into reading whatever it was that you were reading. What was it by the way?" Pearl asked, as they took their seats in the booth. Pearl knew nothing about what she did for a living. Best friend or not, the less people that knew, the better it would be for her.

"Oh, it was just something that Uncle James asked me to take a look at." Reign thought quickly.

"Speaking of, how is he?"

Reign swung her hair over her shoulder and said, "Uncle James is a pain in my ass as always."

"Girl, cut it out," Pearl giggled.

"No, I'm serious. He's always got some shit with him. He's lucky he's my blood uncle or else I wouldn't deal with his funky ass."

Before they ordered, there was breaking news on the diner's TV that had caught everyone's attention. The news reporter was standing in the very same spot that she was in just a few days ago. The reporter waited for the anchors in the station to give her the go ahead.

She nodded her head once and began, "Thank you, Malinda, and you are correct. I'm standing at the scene where victim Kareem White aka Kane was murdered a few nights ago. The body was found by the owner of this store on the corner of Flatbush Ave. He said that when he had gotten here, the scene was as if it was something from the movies. The police do not have any leads on a suspect at this point, but we do know that the killer is the infamous Lipstick Killah. After several bodies have turned up with a crimson red like heart drawn in the victim's wrist. Police have yet to find out who this person is. Male or female? We just don't know. More on this story at eleven. Back to you at the station, Malinda."

After the report was made, everyone went back to what they were doing, including Reign and Pearl. The waitress came over and they both ordered French toast sundaes with cups of coffee. They briefly caught up with each other until Reign's attention was diverted towards the door.

As cool as ever, her target, walked inside of the diner. His caramel colored skin laid smoothly over his bone structure. His deep brown eyes penetrated every face inside of the diner before a waitress came up to him to seat him. His hair was faded on the sides and a bunch of curls rested on top of his head. He stood at six feet three inches and looked to weigh just a bit over two hundred and ten pounds.

'Well this is going to be fun.' Reign thought to herself.

"Reign, hello do you hear me?" Pearl said, snapping her fingers in front of Reign's face.

"I'm sorry, girl, what did you say?"

"I was asking if you wanted to catch a movie later on. I'm tired of being stuck in the house."

"Girl, you are hardly ever in the house. But I guess we can catch a movie. Let me go handle something, really quick. I think I see somebody that I know."

"Girl, you forever saying you see somebody you know," Pearl said, scrunching her face up. She scooped up some ice cream and ate as Reign stood up to walk over to her target.

Normally, she wouldn't walk up to her target and do what she was about to do. Since this would be her last job for a cool minute, why not have some fun? Reign walked by her target's table, swaying her hips to a beat that only she could hear. She glanced at him and saw him watching her every move. Reign walked to the counter and ordered a coffee that she knew that she wouldn't drink. Once she got it, she made sure that she walked in his direction. As expected when she got closer he winked at her and stood in her path.

With a coy smile, she pushed her hair back and tried to walk past him, but he quickly reached his hand out and lightly grabbed her arm.

He said, "You can't be walking past with all that sass and not expect for me to not speak."

Snatching her arm back, she said, "Excuse me, you don't have to touch me for you to speak. Now, let's try this again. Name?"

Jose reached his hand out. Reign looked at him with a smile on her face and took his hand into hers.

He said, "My name is Jose. And yours?"

"My name is Brittany. Nice to meet you, Jose."

"Would you like to join me for a cup of coffee?"

"Actually, my friend and I will be leaving so I will have to take a rain check."

Jose smiled and said, "I peeped that you grabbed a fresh cup of coffee, but it's cool. I'd rather do something other than have a cup of coffee anyway. Take my number down."

Reign took her cell phone out of her back pocket and took his number down. She winked at him and walked back towards Pearl to gather their things to leave. Pearl threw down the money for their food and a tip, then they left out. Once they got to the car, Reign reached her arms out for a hug.

Reign said, "Let me go. I have to get in contact with Uncle James and I'll let you know about catching that movie later on."

"Don't be a bitch and not hit me up. Lately we've both become too busy to have girl time. I really miss our girl time," Pearl said, pouting like a big baby.

"Girl, if you don't fix them soup coolers. I got you," Reign said, causing both of them to giggle. With another quick hug they parted ways. Before Reign pulled away from the diner she called her Uncle and told him that she would make the run for him but that would be the first and last time. He told her to stop by his house before she decided to call it a night to get the directions. Throwing her phone down into her passenger seat, she looked at the diner and went on her way. Only to circle the block to wait for Jose to exit.

## Chapter-Six
## Pearl

Letting out a long sigh as she pulled up to the place she called home, Pearl gathered her things. Pearl skipped the fact that Stanley had moved in a few days prior to her and Reign meeting up. It had been a tough few days for her and she didn't know how her best friend would take to the way her life took a turn for the worst. Of course, she had her new deal with Bobby, but her home life had turned to shit.

Stanley was controlling, so far verbally abusive, and acted like a big ass baby. Pearl thought she was doing him a favor by letting him stay a few days, because from what he said, his place was being fumigated due to the fact that his neighbor was infested with bed bugs. Just that morning, Pearl overheard him talking on the phone and he told whomever he was talking to that the lease expired. He also said that he didn't want to find another spot when Pearl would let him stay. She was shocked to say the least, but this is what her life had become.

Pearl climbed out of her car and walked up the stairs to the front door. Before she could get the key in the lock, the door swung open and Stanley was standing there with a grimace on his face.

"Where have you been?" he asked, scowling at her.

"I told you that I was meeting up with Reign." She brushed past him to get in the door. She wanted to sit down and take her shoes off, the stiletto's she wore on her feet were killing her.

"That was at least four hours ago. When you left the sun was still up. You can't tell me that y'all just now departing from each other."

"No, I've been left her. I decided to ride around to clear my mind and I lost track of time," she said, sighing. She was tired of having to explain her moves especially to someone who she didn't even classify as her man.

Stanley stood in front of her and watched as she took her shoes off. Stanley's normal was to be verbally, mentally, emotionally, and physically abusive to his girlfriends. He tried to control his anger, but he had always been this way and he didn't know how long he'd be able to hold it. To him, with the way she was responding to him was out of line.

"Take your pants off," Stanley demanded.

Pearl looked up at him and said, "Excuse me?"

"I said take your pants off. And while you're at it, you might as well take your panties off too."

Pearl was astounded. Not only did his request confuse her, it was a first for her and she didn't know what to expect from it. She couldn't believe it.

"Stanley, I'm not about to take my pants off, let alone my panties. I don't know what has gotten into you."

Stanley chuckled and with lightning speed, he rushed over to her and pointed his finger into her face. The whites of his eyes had turned red and foam gathered at the corners of his mouth. Pearl pressed into the back of the couch, because that was the only place for her to go.

"I told you to do something, so you might as well just do it. I really don't want this to get ugly. Just take them off and pass them to me." Stanley stared at her for a few seconds and then slowly backed up away from her.

Her heart pounded inside of her chest as she tried not to lose eye contact with this maniac in front of her. She stood up and pulled her pants slowly down her legs. Stanley watched her intently as she reached for her panties next.

"Is this really necessary right now?" she stammered.

"Anything that I tell you to do, whether it makes sense or not is always necessary now finish."

Bending at her waist, she slipped her feet out one at a time and handed her panties to him. She watched him as he raised her panties to his face and sniffed deeply. She watched on as his eyes rolled to the back of his head. *'What the fuck?'* Pearl thought to herself. She had never experienced anything like this before.

"Sit on the couch and open your legs," Stanley growled.

"What?" Pearl decided that she'd had enough.

"You heard exactly what I said. I don't believe that you've been out this long just driving all this time. Your panties smell brand new and I need to smell your pussy," Stanley told her with a straight face.

Pearl's mouth dropped open. Fuck him being a maniac, this fool was straight up insane. Pearl sucked her teeth and began to walk away.

He grabbed her by the arm and pushed her onto the couch looking at her wildly. Throwing her panties onto the other side of the living room, he got on his knees and between her legs. Stanley crawled closer to her and nuzzled his face into her paradise.

He couldn't even lie to himself, her pussy was just as fresh as her panties with just a hint of sweat.

"Are you satisfied? I would like to go upstairs and take a shower and grab something to eat," She spoke, her voice laced with annoyance.

"Yes, I am. But I better not ever find out that you're stepping out on me. There are repercussions if you do so. I don't ever want to have to take it that far."

Pearl didn't even bother to respond. She scurried away with her ass cheeks clapping and thankful that the situation didn't turn drastic. Deep in the back of her mind she knew that she needed to get rid of this dude, but she also knew that if she did, he would make it extremely hard to do. And that's something that she didn't want.

\*\*\*

**Reign**

Reign drove down I-278 West, mad as hell with Uncle James. She could have dealt with the fact that she was delivering a package somewhere in the five boroughs. This fool had her going all the way to Philly. She was going to curse him out something filthy once she made it back and her bread was in the palms of her hands. The drive wasn't the problem, being that it was only an hour and fifteen minutes. It was the fact that he failed to mention how far she was going. She had just gotten onto I-95 when her phone rang. Senaj's number came across the screen placing a big smile on her face. As she answered, she smiled hearing his voice fill her car.

"Hello," she said, with butterflies in her stomach.

"Hello, beautiful." His smooth baritone voice seeped through the speakers.

"Oh, stop it." Was all she could say as she felt her cheeks burning from blushing so hard.

Senaj's laughter filled the car and made Reign feel warm.

"What are you up to?" Senaj asked.

"I am on my way to Philly. I have to come see my aunt, real quick," She quickly lied.

"I guess I'm too late."

"Why, what's up?"

"I had wanted to see if you would like to join me for dinner."

Reign darted her eyes to the clock on her dashboard. It read 8:27 p.m. She calculated that if she could get in and out, she could be back in the city by midnight. They could still grab something to eat, because even on weekdays, most places stayed open late.

"I mean, we could still do dinner. It might be late but I'm pretty sure that I could make it by midnight. There should still be something open," Reign spoke.

He chuckled and said, "There will be something open.

But I'm cooking."

"Ooh, a man that cooks."

"Yes, there are some of us out here. If a man likes to eat he must know how to cook."

"That's the truth."

"So, I'm guessing that it's okay for me to begin to cook?" Senaj asked, crossing his fingers and hoping like hell that she said yes.

"Let me ask you this first. If I wasn't on my way to Philly and you called me, would the food had been done by the time I got there?"

"Of course not, pretty lady. I'm making some of my favorite dishes that my mom used to make. I was hoping to teach you a thing or two."

"Oh, excuse me. I hear that." She giggled.

"I guess I'll see you when you get here. I'm gonna start on this food. I promise I won't make anything extravagant, so everything will be done by the time you get here."

"Sounds like a plan." They said their good byes and hung up. That phone call put Reign in a better mood and just that fast the trip to Philly was the furthest thing from her mind. Just the thought of being with Senaj made her put the pedal to the metal so she could make it back in just enough time.

***

Approximately two hours later, Reign pulled up to her destination and looked around. Almost immediately, she felt like something was off. She brushed it off to nerves because she had a spare tire in her trunk filled with bricks of pure cocaine. Her palms became sweaty and her heart pounded in her chest. She thought maybe she was over thinking the situation and she tried to coax herself into calming down. Pretty soon, an all black Cadillac Escalade pulled up. They flashed their hi-beams, indicating for Reign to get out of her car. At the same time, she got out, a tall muscular man got out and dusted his suit jacket off. The duffel bag that Reign carried was probably heavier than her, but she held onto it like it weighed as much as a new born baby.

"I thought James was coming. But I can't even say that I'm mad that he didn't," muscle man said.

While he was cute, kind of resembling Morris Chestnut, there was not even a smirk on Reign's face. She just wanted to get this done with.

"Where is what you needed to give James?" Reign asked.

The Morris Chestnut lookalike said, "How about we start off with names? Mine is Jameson."

"No need for you to know mine because this will be our only and last meeting."

"Feisty, aren't we?" Jameson said. He leaned against the truck and smiled at Reign.

Reign switched her weight from one foot to the next, getting impatient. Jameson walked up to Reign and she couldn't help but to reach for her pistol that she kept nestled in a harness under her leather jacket.

"Don't come any closer. I just need what I came here for, James." Ice was laced in her words.

"Ahh, you're Reign, James' niece," Jameson said, smiling once again. "You look different in person compared to the pictures that I've seen."

The first thought that popped into Reign's head was *'Why is Uncle James talking about and showing pictures of me to people?'*

"I have things to do," Reign said.

"Do you know that you are supposed to be dead right now?" Jameson asked, walking closer to Reign.

She didn't believe a word that he said. Why would she?

She didn't know him from Adam. Reign gripped her pistol tighter, ready to let it talk. The only reason why she didn't was because she wanted to know what he was talking about.

"What are you talking about?" Reign asked.

"I hate to be the one to bear bad news, but your uncle told me to have you killed tonight. After you delivered this package. He didn't tell me it was his own niece. Tsk, tsk," Jameson said, shaking his head.

"You're lying," Reign said.

"If you allow me to get closer, I can show you the text messages that he sent me just an hour ago."

Curiosity got the best of her and she slowly lowered her gun. Jameson pulled his phone from his pocket and proceeded to show Reign the messages. She wished she could say Jameson was lying. She didn't want to believe that a complete stranger was showing her this bullshit from her uncle. Her heart broke with every message that she read.

"Why are you telling me this?" Reign asked, dropping the duffel bag on the ground.

"One, because you are too beautiful to be laying in somebody's dirt. Two, I want to give you an offer, I'm pretty sure you can't refuse."

"I'm pretty sure I'm not interested."

"We'll see."

Reign rolled her eyes as he proceeded to tell her his offer. She of course thought he was crazy for even saying what it was he wanted from her. She left the meeting with her thoughts heavy and at that moment, she thought that death was better than anything at this point.

# Mimi

## Chapter – Seven
## Senaj & Reign

Senaj was happier than a kid in a candy store. His music played, and he danced around his kitchen. He had gotten a call from both of his boys asking if he wanted to come out, but he declined. They clowned him after they found out the reason why he was declining was because of his date with Reign. The clowning got worse once they found out that he was staying in and cooking for her. The music from his phone cut off, indicating that he had a call coming through. He dried his hands while looking at the screen. He smiled when he saw that it was Reign calling.

"I hope you're calling because you're on your way here and you need directions," Senaj said, with a big smile on his face.

"Senaj, I don't need the address nor the directions. I already know where you live. I'm calling because I'm going to have to take a rain check. I'm so sorry," Reign spoke.

Senaj could tell that she was truly saddened about the change in plans.

"Oh?" he simply said, his hopes dwindling down to nothing.

"I'm sorry, something came up. I have to meet with my Uncle. But I promise I'm going to make it up. I know you made a wonderful dinner."

"It's no big thing. Only thing is that tomorrow I go back to doing my residency. It's going to be a little more difficult to catch up with me."

"That's okay with me. I could tell that you're a good catch, so I'll wait it out."

That brought a huge grin to his face and he couldn't front. He liked what he heard. He said, "Do what you got to do, beautiful."

With that they hung up the phone and Senaj sent a text letting his boys know that they were more than welcome to come and grab some food once they called it a night. He finished cooking, ate, showered and headed to bed.

\*\*\*

It was close to two o' clock once Senaj had finally made his way into a deep slumber. He was oblivious to the figure that was waiting in the shadows. Once the figure heard his light snores, they moved to the bed, took their shoes off and slid in next to Senaj. Once he felt movement in his bed, he jumped up in fear that he was being robbed. Once his eyes adjusted, he realized that it was Reign. A smile as beautiful as the first time he's actually seen her smile.

"What? How did you get in? How did you know where I lived?" He fired questions at her while eyeing her. Their connection was out of this world, but he didn't know her from Adam and Reign gaining access, didn't sit well with him.

"I have my ways. I couldn't wait to find out when would be the next time I see you," Reign whispered.

"Trust me, I would have tried my hardest to make some time. Even if it would be for five minutes."

"You're the sweetest. When is your graduation?"

"Next year in May."

"Six months from now. Are you ready?"

"As ready as I'll ever be. I've wanted this my whole life."

She looked up at Senaj as he spoke passionately about becoming a doctor. She realized that she never really truly thought about going to college to become anything. She was distraught after the passing of her father that she dismissed college and jumped head on into the business.

"Did you hear what I just said?" Senaj asked, breaking her thoughts.

"No, I'm sorry. I was thinking about something. What did you say?" Reign responded honestly.

"I asked you about your parents. When we were in Central Park, I told you about mine. You had to go before I was able to ask about yours."

Reign sighed. Not even while she was dating Josiah did she mention her parents. Except one time when they first started dating. She simply told him that they were deceased, and it was never brought up again. Reign cleared her throat and said, "My mom passed when I was four, due to cancer and my dad passed on my graduation day. As soon as I had my diploma in my hand, I turned to see him grabbing at his chest. He was gone by the time we got to the hospital. Heart attack, a massive one."

Senaj grabbed her into a hug and kissed her forehead. Reign hadn't dropped a tear since the day of her father's burial. She didn't know why but as soon as she felt his arms wrap around her, the tears fell, unwanted.

"I'm sorry to hear that," Senaj said.

"No, it's okay. I've come to grips about it. I wish I just had a little more time with them, especially my mom. I only have a few memories with her, but my dad made sure that he spoke about her often and showed me pictures of her. While that is great, there is nothing like spending time with her." Reign couldn't believe how choked up she was about it. Her body shook as she sniffled and tried to keep her tears at bay.

"Stay right here," Senaj said.

"Yeah, like I'm gonna go somewhere." She giggled.

Senaj side eyed her and left out of his room. Walking down the hall to the bathroom, he ran hot water inside of his tub. Reaching under his sink cabinet, he grabbed his lavender and chamomile scented bubble bath and Epsom salt. He poured in a generous amount and walked back towards his room.

# Mimi

"Get up," he ordered.

"What? What are you doing?" Reign asked, placing the remote on the bed.

"I promise I won't bite," he said, with a bright smile.

Reign rolled her eyes and reluctantly grabbed Senaj's hand. She was shocked that he drew her a bath. She looked at him in his eyes and stood on her tip toes holding onto the back of his neck. Pulling him closer to her, she kissed his lips. Senaj closed his eyes and accepted the kiss, sparks flew between them as if they were experiencing their first kiss all over again. For a few seconds they stopped and just looked at each other.

Each had separate thoughts running through their heads but at that moment all they were worried about was their lips connecting again. His hands wrapped around her tiny waist and palmed both of her ass cheeks in his hands. Reign's body was melting all over his hands, as his touch made her moist. She jumped up and he caught her, causing her legs to swing around his body. Senaj walked over to the toilet and sat down, doing so as their lips didn't move from each other. Reign felt his dick slowly coming to life and if she had to admit to herself, she was scared.

He broke the kiss first. Reign looked on, wanting to ask him why he stopped. Using her thumb, she wiped her lipstick from his lips. Senaj smirked and slowly took her shirt off and ran his hands across her smooth skin. He lifted her up, causing her to place her feet on the ground. Senaj helped her out of her pants and was blown away by her body. There were a few scrapes and scars, but he was still in awe.

Usually confident when she was alone, but she couldn't help but to feel self-conscious in front of Senaj. She got ready to question his gaze, but was cut short when he placed soft kisses onto her stomach.

"Come on. I'll give you some privacy while you finish undressing," Senaj said, standing and making his way out of the bathroom.

"What if I want you to join?" Reign asked, looking up at him bashfully.

He couldn't help but to smile. Senaj took his clothes off, hoping that she would ask that. Reign stripped out of her panties and bra allowing Senaj to get inside of the tub.

For fifteen minutes, they sat in the tub relaxing. Not saying anything, sorting through their own thoughts.

"You ready? I don't want to fall asleep in the tub," he joked.

"Yes, I'm ready. Cause I damn sure was ready to do just that."

Rinsing the soap from their bodies, they grabbed towels and made their way into the bedroom. They moisturized their bodies and climbed inside of the bed.

"I'm really glad that you came, even if you broke a law." Senaj chuckled.

*'If only you knew how many laws I break daily.'* She thought. Instead she said, "Get some sleep."

With a kiss he did just that. They were both exhausted from their day, so calling it an early night, they passed out within minutes of climbing into the bed.

\*\*\*

Senaj was awake at promptly eight-thirty in the morning. A smile spread across his face, as he remembered his night with Reign. Rolling over, he prepared himself to throw his arm over Reign's body, but she wasn't there. He sat straight up in his bed and looked around his room, wondering if it was all a dream. Climbing out of his bed, he opened his room door and heard movement in the kitchen. He made his way towards the kitchen and saw Reign busying herself with heating up the food from last night. A smile grew upon his face as he watched her move about with such ease in one of his shirts, which swallowed her whole.

"Good morning, beautiful," he said, almost scaring the shit out of Reign. She almost dropped the glass plate she was holding. Not expecting Senaj to wake up as early as she did, she allowed herself to let her guards down and get comfortable in his environment. For once.

"Sheesh! You can't creep upon me like that. Good morning," Reign said, placing a kiss on his lips.

Senaj reached around her body and squeezed her ass, causing her panties to get moist. His dick instantly got hard.

"How about we put that food on hold for a few minutes?"

Reign removed her arms from around his neck and said, "That's all you got? A few minutes?"

Senaj smirked and said, "Hell no. I can show you better than I can tell you."

Reign grabbed Senaj's hand, as she led him to his bedroom. Once inside, she instructed Senaj to lay down on the bed and she climbed on top of him. Leaning down she placed kisses on his neck that trailed up to his face. Senaj reached above him and took her shirt off. Holding her at the small of her back, he rolled her under him. Using both of his hands, he squeezed both of her titties, before he used his tongue to circle her nipples, causing her to arch her back. Senaj loved the way her body reacted to his touch.

Slipping one of his hands down to her love box, he rubbed his finger up and down her slit. His fingers became instantly coated in her juices. Reign moaned against his lips, as she felt herself ready to explode on his fingers. Removing his lips from hers, he placed kisses on her body leading down to her pussy. Reign didn't think she could contain herself. Senaj spread her legs with his shoulders and laid flat on his stomach, while using his index and middle finger to spread her lips. He took in the sight of her pretty pink pussy, as it glistened with wetness. Senaj kissed her swollen clit and eased his finger inside of her. Senaj circled her clit with his tongue, adding the right amount of pressure to cause immense pleasure.

"Mmm, yes!" Reign moaned out, rotating her hips.

"Shh. Just enjoy it," Senaj whispered against her pussy. Reign bit her bottom lip because she didn't know how she was going to be quiet when his tongue was feeling oh so right on her clit.

His tongue moved faster over her clit, causing Reign to have the biggest climax that she'd ever had. He continued to please her, having her shake with each orgasm she had. Reign had to push his head away from her once she'd had enough. Senaj simply chuckled, as he removed his body from between her legs. As he made his way to the dresser, he eyed her like a lion stalking his prey. He stroked himself watching her pussy glistened.

"You see something you like Daddy?" she asked. Opening her legs further and even though her clit was tender, she rubbed it in circular motions; teasing him.

"Oh yeah, I definitely do." Senaj placed a condom on his dick and made his way to the bed.

Reign giggled like she was a kid in a candy store. Senaj grabbed both of Reign's legs and threw them onto his shoulders. Moving his pelvis and without using his hands, he maneuvered his penis to slide his head up and down her slit. Reign moaned while grabbing both of her breasts and squeezed both of her nipples, which caused huge amounts of pleasure to coarse through her body.

Senaj placed his dick in the opening of her pussy and slowly glided his penis in her; struggling just a bit due to her tightness. She was so tight that he thought that he was going to bust soon as he got through. Once he was in all the way, he paused for a few seconds to catch his composure. He slowly moved in and out of Reign, feeling like he was in heaven. Reign felt the same way and she didn't understand how he was able to take her to such heights that she couldn't do herself. They hadn't even been at it for a full five minutes before she was shaking and nutting all over him. Covering her face, she couldn't help but to feel embarrassed.

"I've never felt pussy this good. You got some magic on you," He whispered in her ear as he began to move faster.

Reign's moans drove him crazy and he was ready to bust. Senaj pulled himself out and told her to lay on her stomach. Reign did what he asked and hiked her ass in the air. Her arch was just right as he slid inside of her, he balanced himself by placing his hands in the dip of her back and moved in and out of her, hitting her spot in just the right way.

"Oh my God Senaj! I'm gonna cum all over this dick!" Reign moaned, loving every inch that he pounded inside of her.

"Girl, you better not. Wait for me," he said, through gritted teeth.

He picked his pace up, not wanting to make her wait for too long. The blood pumped into his dick as he stroked her harder. Reign's moans turned into screams of pleasure, as she waited for him.

"Senaj, baby, I don't know how much longer I can wait." She moaned.

With a smack on her ass that left a hand print, he told her to cum. Soon as she got the green light, she squirted all over him, the bed, and herself. Senaj continued to pump inside of her as he came. He didn't stop until he was drained, and all his kids were swimming around inside of the condom. He collapsed on top of her and kissed the back of her neck and rolled off her. After a few moments, Reign began to speak.

"What time you have to be at the hospital?" she asked, willing her body to stop shaking.

Looking at his cell phone, he realized it was now going

on eleven. He said, "At two."

Reign sat up and began to stretch. Exposing her breasts, Senaj grabbed one into his hand and softly squeezed. He didn't want this moment to end because he knew reality was about to hit him and he didn't know when he'd be able to see her again.

"Don't mean to hit it and run, but I have some things to take care of," Reign said, and kissed his lips.

"Just use me like I'm a piece of meat," Senaj spoke, trying to sound offended.

Reign laughed and said, "Not at all. I wish that we could live in this moment forever, but unfortunately reality is here. And I can only promise that we will see each other again."

Senaj agreed, as he watched her move about his room throwing her clothes on. When she was done, he placed his feet inside of his boxers and walked her to the door. They kissed each other like it was their last kiss and before Senaj knew it, Reign disappeared.

# Mimi

# Chapter – Eight
## Pearl

If shit couldn't get any worse for Pearl, it did. She had a meeting with her label and they told her that, without much of an explanation, they had decided not to sign her. At the time that Bobby told her that they decided not to sign her, she drew her own conclusion and figured that since the label had recently been on the news for a drug bust, they made that decision. Maybe they wanted to get the cops off their backs for a little while before they decided to sign her or anyone else for that matter. This was the only reason that popped into Pearl's mind as to why they changed their minds. She was so depressed, because for the longest all she wanted was to be signed to major label and once she could almost taste it, it was taken right from under her feet.

Pearl was relaxing on the couch watching re-runs of Love and Hip-Hop Atlanta, when Stanley came prancing inside of the house with a bunch of bags from various stores at the mall. Stanley was the last person she wanted to see. So, with a roll of her eyes, she directed her attention to the TV and scooped some ice cream into her mouth.

"No hey honey? How was your day?" Stanley asked, while taking a seat on the couch next to Pearl.

"I'm not quite exactly in a hey honey, how was your day, kind of mood," Pearl said, while still looking at the TV.

"I don't know what crawled up your ass, but you better fix that shit! I mean fix it right now!" Stanley shouted in Pearl's face.

Pearl was tired of hearing his mouth. She exhaled and jumped from the couch and yelled, "This has been the most horrible day for me, one that I've had in a long while! While you're out gallivanting and spending money, I've received the news that I was dropped from the label, that I didn't even get a chance to sign the contract for! You're not making things any easier with your "I am God and what I says go" attitude!"

Before Pearl knew it, her head snapped back and began to sting, as she felt the burning sensation on her full lips. She stood in shock and looked at Stanley who had a slight smirk on his face. Touching her lip where it burned, she removed her hand to see that she was bleeding.

"Did you just fucking hit me?" she asked.

Without missing a beat, Stanley said, "I damn sure did and if you don't take your yelling ass somewhere, I'll do it again. Try me if you want to, Pearl."

Moments passed before Stanley realized what was happening. Pearls scream was so loud and high pitched that it could have burst someone's ear drums. She ran at him with full force and began raining blows on him, getting the best of him. He stood from the couch and wrapped his arms around her waist. Pulling her body towards him, he picked her up and suplexed her into the wooden coffee table. Pain rippled through her body and she had no choice but to lay on her back with broken wood surrounding her.

Stanley stood over her with his teeth showing, like he was a dog growling. He said, "Let you try that shit again and I'm gonna make an example out of your ass! Now get your ass up off that floor and get the fuck in the kitchen and cook a nigga some dinner!"

Pearl couldn't believe what the fuck just happened. She couldn't make sense of it and she so badly wanted to jump on him and continue to attack him. Her gut told her not to do such a thing again. She was pretty sure that he would stick to his word and fuck her up something bad.

It took her some time to get up off the floor, but she managed to make it to the bathroom. Her lip was busted something crazy and swollen. She refused to let any tears fall from her eyes, but Pearl couldn't help it. As she cleaned her face up, she thought about calling Reign. She shook the thought from her mind and just proceeded to go inside of the kitchen to cook for Stanley. She made him a dinner worthy for a king and so many times she wanted to slip just enough bleach inside of the water of the pilaf rice that she was making him. She made T-Bone steak, pilaf rice, brussels sprouts, and sat him a beer next to his food. She let him know that the food was done and decided to just call it a night. She took a shower and got comfortable in her favorite cozy pajamas. Before she knew it, she passed out.

Several hours later, Pearl woke up because Stanley was making a ton of noise inside of the bedroom. She played possum as she watched him move about. He staggered over to the dresser where he rummaged through her dresser and grabbed something. Stanley got undressed and walked over to where Pearl was laying, causing her to slap her eyes shut.

"Pearl? Baby? Are you sleep?" Stanley asked, looking down at her.

He couldn't help but to smile because besides him being abusive, he actually did love her. He wanted to be a changed man, but he didn't know how to escape his mentality in order to do so. Stroking himself, he reached down to caress her face.

Still playing possum, Pearl moved her face away from him slightly causing him to fully shake her.

"Stanley, what do you want?" Pearl asked, irritated.

She made the mistake in turning her back to him and it ignited a fire in Stanley that he had never experienced before. He grabbed Pearl by her shirt and dragged her to the floor, where she immediately began kicking and screaming. He lost his grip and she tried to scramble away, but she didn't get very far because he was right over her grabbing her by the hair.

"Who do you think you are, turning your back on me? I was just trying to show your ass some affection!"

"Stanley, stop! You're hurting me!" Pearl yelled.

Stanley punched her in the back of the head and yelled, "I'll stop when I feel like stopping. To think I was just really thinking about becoming a changed man for you. I love you, Pearl, don't you see that?"

"Yes, I do, baby. But Stanley, you're hurting me."

Pearl's pleas fell on deaf ears, as she grabbed at his fingers to let her hair go. All that did was piss him off, causing him to land a blow to her face. Instinctively, her hands went to her face as she felt warm liquid pouring from the same exact spot that it did a few hours ago.

"You think I care? That's what you get for turning your back on me. Now get your ass up and come suck my dick."

"You busted my lip *again*! Hell no! And as a matter of fact, you could get your shit and get the fuck out of my house!" Pearl said, getting up from off the floor.

Stanley's eyes bulged from his head, as he watched Pearl storm off to the connected bathroom. She looked at herself in the mirror and grew angry at the sight that she saw. Stanley walked to the bathroom door and stood by the door and watched Pearl clean her face.

"Pearl, I'm sorry, baby. I don't know what has gotten into me, lately. I could be stressed out, I don't know. I really do love you and wish that we could work it out."

Pearl stopped cleaning her face. Unfortunately for her, she did love him. She had loved him way before the abuse had started. The sincerity in his voice had her ready to forget that she was standing in front of him, bloody from his hands no less. She couldn't help but to feel hopeful.

"Do you really mean that, Stanley?" she asked. She wanted to believe him so bad, but she just couldn't. At least not fully. He would have to prove to her that he wanted to change.

"Hell no, bitch! I want some pussy!" He yelled and grabbed her by the neck, dragging her back into the room. He threw her onto the bed and climbed on top of her.

# Lipstick Killah

She kicked and swung, until he grabbed her wrists and got in her face. He threatened to hit her again if she didn't stop moving. By this time, Stanley's dick was rock hard, and he couldn't help but to yearn to feel her insides.

"If you move when I get off of you, I promise, you're not going to like the outcome. I advise you to stay still," Stanley warned.

Tears fell down the sides of her face and she was frozen in place. She didn't want to piss him off even further. Stanley tugged at her pants and watched her, daring her to make a move.

"Please don't do this, Stanley," Pearl cried.

"You had to be a bitch about it. We could have been doing this the right way, but you want to make it hard."

Pearl laid there and went back and forth with herself if she wanted to fight. She knew if she did, then it wouldn't be any good on her part. After all, he was a man and was physically stronger then she was. In her mind, it was flight or fight, she knew she had to. Pearl watched as he bent over to take her legs from out of her pants and once one leg was out, she raised her foot up and slammed it hard into his face. His hand automatically shot up to his face, as he fell flat on his ass. Pearl sat up on the bed and a surge of adrenaline rushed through her body. Stanley sitting on the floor helpless, caused Pearl to realize that if she was to have done this earlier on, she wouldn't be in the predicament that she was in now. Jumping from the bed, she stood over him and with all her might, she hit him with a left hook and then a right hook.

"You thought you was just about to rape me in here! One thing for certain and two things for sure, you got me fucked up! I let this shit go on for far too long!" Pearl yelled, as she circled him and taunted him.

Stanley sat covering his face and he couldn't help but to feel the rage building up on him. Pearl didn't know what kind of trouble she was in. The more she walked and taunted, the faster he was able to get over the initial shock of her actually fighting back.

"Now you ain't so tough cause I done caught your ass slipping! You not so tough! Bi-" Pearl was cut off by Stanley grabbing her by the legs and stood up causing her head to hit the ceiling before slamming her body onto the bed.

He slammed her so hard that the box spring underneath the mattress broke. As Pearl yelped out in pain, Stanley stood over her with a snarl on his face. His heart rate increased, as he was now at his boiling point. At this point all he saw was red. Pearl tried to move, but she couldn't. Stanley grabbed her by her legs and dragged her off the bed.

"You caught me slipping right?" Stanley snarled. He straddled her body and wrapped his hands around her neck.

"No. Please, Stanley, stop." She struggled to get out, as she began to lose oxygen.

"Oh, now it's Stanley, stop. All you had to do was give me the pussy." He had gotten close to her to make sure that she heard him.

When he moved away, he removed one hand from her neck and with his big meaty closed fist, he punched her square in the nose. Instantly her nose leaked blood, causing her to try to scream out in pain, but it only came out as choking sounds. Stanley still had his hand around her neck. Using his free hand, he unzipped his pants and searched around in his pants for his penis, that had surprisingly stayed hard throughout the ordeal.

Pearl whimpered, as she went in and out of consciousness. By now, she just accepted the fact that he was going to strangle her to death. She felt him trying to get his dick inside of her but was unsuccessful, due to her being dry.

Stanley spit on the tips of his fingers to provide some

type of lubricant. Once he was able to penetrate her, he released his hand and began to pump away. Pearl welcomed the air that she was pumping into her lungs.

"See all you had to do was give me this sweet pussy," Stanley said, breathing heavy into her ear. Tears cascaded down her face, Stanley watched, mad that she was making him seem like he was hurting her. He balled his fist up and sucker punched her, knocking the wind out of her.

He didn't stop there, because he made her turn over onto her stomach where he did the same thing to her ass, that he did to her pussy. He entered her asshole roughly, causing a searing pain to ripple through her body. He couldn't take the sound of her cries, so he began punching her in her back and her sides, yelling for her to shut her mouth. He only stopped hitting her once she did shut up. The assault on her ass didn't stop though. He pumped away roughly, until he was able to bring himself near climax. He hurriedly flipped her over onto her back and grabbed her by the hair and jerked off on her face.

"Ahh!" he yelled, as he watched his thick cum splash onto her face and mixed in with the blood. Stanley pushed her body onto the floor, causing her head to bounce off the floor. He stood over her while placing his dick into his pants.

"Go clean yourself up and take your ass to bed," Stanley said, simply walking away to go sleep on the couch.

*'Lord why didn't you take me when you had the chance to?'* Pearl thought as she laid on the floor, feeling the lowest that she had ever felt in her life. How did she ever become so weak that she had allowed for her life to turn into shit?

Growing up she had never experienced domestic violence and not one of her old relationships was domestic violence. She wanted to be strong enough to be able to leave, but she didn't have anywhere to go, and her mother lived all the way on the other side of the country. Pearl knew she deserved better, but Stanley made sure that she would always need him, he controlled everything.

Pearl got up and walked into the bathroom. Filling the tub up with hot water, she took her clothes off. Once the tub was full, she eased inside of the tub and let the water soothe her aching body. She vowed one day, that she would have the courage to leave and she only hoped that it would be one day soon.

# Chapter -Nine
## Reign

Reign's head was spinning with what Jameson had told her. Before going to see Senaj, she went to her Uncle James' house to drop off his money and to get her portion. The surprise that was written on his face when he opened the door and saw his niece. He tried to clean it up fast, but Reign caught it and didn't say anything about it. Reign invited herself in and took a seat at the kitchen table.

James followed her, racking his brain as to how she was still alive. Once inside the kitchen, he placed the bag on the table and gave her percentage. It was eerily quiet until James asked about the trip.

"It was smooth." Was Reign's short reply.

"Um, have you started that job that I gave you the file on?" James asked, unsure of what to exactly say. He was confused, and Jameson was going to catch hell.

"I actually ran into him while out with Pearl. He introduced himself to me. With you sending me to Philly, I couldn't get a chance to check his movements yet." Reign spoke, finally making eye contact.

She couldn't help to feel the betrayal. *'How could I be so loyal to such a snake?'* She thought. James had been her favorite uncle. No scratch that, her only uncle and person from her family that she fucked with. Once her parents died, the money stopped coming in, and they stopped fucking with her. James was the only person that she had trusted and now, not at all.

"I think you should get on that as soon as possible. You don't want the Mexican Cartel to be after you."

"They won't be."

"How could you be so sure?" James asked, zipping up the small duffel bag that contained Reign's portion of the money.

"You forget who my dad was? After all, he was your brother. So, you should know that I can hold my own."

"Reign, even you know that most times than none, he was always in some shit that was hard for him to get out of."

"While that may be true, I am almost near perfect when I'm on a job. Sure, I get a few bumps and bruises, but I've, and I'm knocking on wood, have yet to be stabbed, shot, or hospitalized."

James exhaled and said, "Reign, just get the job done and efficiently. You need to get ghost soon."

It took everything in Reign to not expose what she knew. She wanted to rip him apart, limb to limb. Reign simply nodded her head and grabbed her bag. She told Uncle James to have a good night. Once she left, she took her money to her stash spot and made her way to see Senaj.

***

For the past few days, Reign couldn't help but to think about everything that Jameson had said. Her thoughts flashed back to the night she went to Philly to make the drop for James.

*Reign read the text message conversation between her Uncle James and Jameson. James' order for Jameson to kill Reign was simple and straight to the point. When Jameson would ask James why, he wouldn't answer. Jameson heard stories from James about Reign but had never see her. In photo nor in person. It was a surprise to him that Reign was actually in front of him and he was so captured by her beauty, that he came up with a plan. For him, sparing her life, she would have to work for him. He knew how precise she was with her work and he would pay her handsomely if she agreed. Before they departed Jameson told her that before the drop was scheduled to be made, he met with James for drinks and James' lips got loose with each drink. James told him the reason why he wanted Reign killed.*

# Lipstick Killah

*A while back, Reign had done a job and she had killed an important figure on the streets. He was James' plugs nephew and when he'd gotten wind of it, he wanted her head on a platter. Around that same time, James had found out that Reign was sitting on close to seven million dollars from her father K.B. James' wanted it, but he didn't know where it was at. James' plug had given him a call letting him know that he knew it was Reign that had whacked his nephew. He told James to bring Reign to him, but James had other plans. He was going to have somebody run down on Reign and torture her until she gave them the information that he needed. While James' plug sat on money on top of money, he couldn't turn down the half that James promised him if he agreed to let James take care of it. Little did James know, Reign knew nothing about where the seven million was stashed.*

She knew now that there was seven million dollars stashed for her and she needed to get to it before her snake ass uncle got to it. Reign finally pushed the thoughts to the back of her head as she got ready to follow Jose. Tonight, she planned on getting the job done and taking a leave from the business. She needed to ponder things over and knew she wouldn't be on point if she picked up another job with all this on her mind.

Reign made her way to her closet as she looked through her large selection of black clothes. She decided to put on some black jeans that had zippers over the pockets, a black tank top, her leather Steve Madden jacket, and all black ankle booties with a low chunky heel. She did her hair in a low ponytail with a swoop bang and of resembling the hair style that Aaliyah wore in Romeo Must Die. In the small of her back, she held a .22 and underneath her jacket was a holster that carried two nines. Attached to her booties were ninja stars which passed off as a part of the design for the shoe. Last but not least, she had her trusty razor blade, hidden on the inside of her cheek. Just in case if she was ever in a desperate situation.

Checking the time, she noticed that she had to hurry up and leave in order to catch Jose leaving the strip club. As she made her way to her garage, she couldn't help but to think about Senaj. A smile came across her face but soon disappeared. She needed for him not to pass through her mind so that she could stay focused. Shaking her head, she climbed into her Audi, opened the garage door, and flew down the street like a bat out of hell.

Twenty minutes later, Reign was pulling up to a hole in the wall strip club called Sugars. Outside of the club was quiet but you could hear the bass of the music playing. Turning her car off, she sat in the shadows to access her surroundings. Two hours passed and out stumbled Jose. He was quite drunk and had a stripper on each arm. They clumsily walked towards Jose's car while laughing and they all got in. Reign waited until they did to start up her car. Jose didn't so much as start the car yet causing Reign to sit there in wonderment. She wanted to follow him to his spot and do the deed there. She had already wasted two hours waiting for him to come out.

Finally, after an extra twenty minutes, Jose started his car and pulled off.

Reign waited a full minute, to give him time to be a head of her and then she pulled off. She could have easily set camp out front of his house, but she liked the thrills of cat and mouse. He was the mouse and she was the cat. They finally arrived at his second home, which Reign referred to as his hoeing house, in Staten Island and Reign played it off and continued on down the block and parked.

She waited fifteen minutes and climbed out of her car. From the case that she had gotten from James, she knew that he had four security details stationed around his house. Two in the back and two in the front. Reign knew that he wouldn't be paying attention to the cameras due to the fact that he was going to be occupied.

Walking to the trunk of her car, she ran her hand across the floor of the trunk to find the keypad to her hidden compartment. She entered her six-digit pass code and then laid her index finger on the screen so that she could gain access to her weaponry. Taking her guns out of their holsters, she placed them inside of the compartment. She left her .22 in the small of her back and her ninja stars on her shoes. Inside of her compartment she had her newly purchased rose gold Maxim 9's that had a built-in suppressor on it. She'd never used them and tonight she was putting these bad boys to use. She took the bullets from its box and loaded the magazine's. Closing her trunk, she made her way up the block towards the house before Jose's. She stuck to the shadows as she scaled alongside of the house, staying close to being unseen as possible.

From Jose's neighbor's backyard, she hid in some bushes and watched as the two beefy security guards sat on some lawn chairs while smoking cigars and talking shit about their boss. Reign was grateful that there were only bushes separating the property. She laid on her stomach and aimed at the beefier security guard head. She slowed her breathing down and counted to three squeezing the trigger, her bullet made its target spraying the other security guard with blood and thoughts. Reign didn't allow the second security guard to react and she splashed his thoughts where he sat.

Reign waited for a few moments before she came from the bushes and crept to the front. She would have missed the two guards if one of them hadn't said something. Reign stood still and listened before she decided to make her move.

"You know that fool is going to be high as a kite tonight. It's a wonder that he even made it home," The guard that was closer to Reign said.

"Man, that's his business. He's lucky that I need this money. Malika is going to be having my junior soon and I just want to make things light for her. I want to make sure that they have everything that they need," The second one said.

Reign didn't want to kill the father to be. Her mind worked over time as she thought about whether she should let him live or not. She raised her arms and leveled the guns at the guard who had spoken first. Tapping both triggers at the same time dropping him instantly. The father to be pushed from against the wall and looked around aiming his gun from side to side. Reign popped out from out of her hiding spot, causing the guard to aim in her direction.

"Wait!" She yelled, in a hushed whisper. She put her hands up in surrender, but she was still holding her guns.

"Why should I? You just popped my partner and probably the other two in the back," he snarled.

"Listen, if you really wanted to shoot me, I wouldn't have gotten the chance to say anything. I need for you to hear me out," Reign spoke.

"What if I don't want to? What if I just leave your ass here stinking?"

"You would have done so by now. Listen, I'm just here to do a job and that's it. I overheard you talking about you were about to be a father and that's why I let you stay alive. All you have to do is let me do my job, I'm not here for money or drugs but if you want both or either or you could leave with it," Reign explained, finally putting her arms down.

"What exactly are you here to do?" He too put his gun down.

"The less you know the better. All you have to do is let me inside, just watch to make sure no one comes. You come in and do whatever it is that you want to I'll take the tapes so neither one of us are spotted."

Reign saw him bounce the idea around his head for a while. He knew Jose was sitting on a lot of money. He had been around Jose for the past six months and he had gotten close enough for him to know exactly where his safe was.

A few months prior, Wesley happened to see the code to the safe and since then he had made plans to hit it. He just didn't know that, that day was his lucky day. Wesley couldn't pass up the offer and he held his hand out for Reign to grab so he could help her up the side of the porch.

"Don't take too long," he replied.

"I never do."

Wesley opened the door for Reign. She quickly surveyed the living room area from the foyer and quickly decided that he wasn't downstairs, it was too quiet. She slowly made her way upstairs and listened for any activity that indicated his location. She faintly heard the women giggling, as she made her way down the hallway. As she drew closer to the prize door, she raised her guns in front of her. Raising her foot, she kicked the door, startling the trio.

The three of them were naked sniffing coke off each other. Reign aimed her guns at the two women sending bullets straight to their hearts. Jose was so high that he couldn't register what was going on. She ran up on him and jumped onto the bed, kicking him in his chest. The ninja stars that were on her shoes sliced his chest up to the white meat. He touched his chest and looked down at his hand. Reign stood over him and pointed both guns at him.

"You're the chick from the diner," he said, before Reign pulled the trigger.

One bullet to the heart, the other to the head. She jumped off of the bed and ran around the house looking for his security system. Finding it in the basement, she extracted the disk that was recording and destroyed the equipment. Going back into the living room, she trashed the room and walked back onto the porch. Wesley stood there looking at her like she was crazy.

"Being that I let you live, I'm going to need your ID," Reign stated, with her hand out.

Wesley chuckled and then said, "I won't snitch."

"Your mouth says that, but I can't be too careful. I already went against one of my biggest rules. Please don't make me regret it. Hand it over or you leave me no choice but to take it."

Wesley saw the seriousness in her face and decided to play fair. Wesley was a nigga from the streets and wasn't a snitch, but he had no choice but to play it her way. He understood where she was coming from. He went into his cargo pants pocket and took his ID out of his wallet.

"Let the circumstances had been different, Ma, I would have had you bent over somewhere," he said, with a smile.

Reign smiled ever so sweetly and walked closer to him to only hit him on the side of his neck, a pressure point. She backed up as he fell to the ground, holding his neck.

"No, you wouldn't have," she said and walked away.

"Jesus, woman!" Was the last thing Reign heard, while turning down the street to her car. Placing a kiss on each gun, she placed them back inside of her trunk and locked them back up. Climbing in, she sent a text that simply said, *Disposed.*

Her night was complete, and she couldn't wait until she got home to take a shower, eat, and get some much-needed rest. She would wake up to her account looking nice and she would worry about dealing with her uncle at a later date.

## Chapter - Ten
## Senaj

It had been a week since he last saw Reign, but they texted and talked everyday whenever Senaj was free. It was getting closer to Senaj's graduation and the end of his program. He had started to become more available but was under a lot of pressure. While he enjoyed his residency, he couldn't wait for it to be over.

Senaj was off and decided that he would make a trip out to go see his brother. He hadn't seen him in months and didn't mind taking the hour and a half ride out to Fishkill Correctional Facility. His brother didn't know that he was coming so it would be quite a surprise.

Senaj left early that Friday morning and made it just in time for visiting hours to start. He went through the lengthy process of being searched and after ten minutes he was in the waiting area waiting for his brother to come out. Chi searched the room to see who was visiting him, until his eyes landed on his baby brother. A huge smile spread his face as he walked up to him and took him into a bear hug.

"Senaj! If it wasn't so frowned upon in here to show emotion. I'd let these tears flow more than Niagara Falls," Chi said into his ear.

"I understand. I know it's been a while since I've seen you, but I've gotten so busy lately," Senaj spoke once they broke their hug.

"Yeah, I know. You too busy becoming a doctor to check on your only brother." Chi acted as if he was offended but couldn't help but to crack a smile.

"Oh please! I know you can't do much behind these walls, but what have you been up to?"

"Nothing, man. They got me in here working, doing laundry and shit. I'm just trying to do what I got to do to get out. Oh, and speaking of, come Monday, I have a

Mimi

meeting with the parole board. I need to be a free man again. I've yet to experience life on the outside," Chi said, sounding heartbroken. After all, he did get locked up at the age of twenty-five.

"There is nothing out in this free world that's even remotely exciting, big bro."

"You a damn lie. Just 'cause I'm locked away don't mean that I don't know what these girl's out here looking like. Ass and titties for days. They didn't have them like that when I was out," Chi spoke, with laughter.

Senaj joined in and said, "So when you go in front of the parole board, what's going to happen?"

"I had to write a book damn near, explaining to these damn crackers that I've learned my lesson and I'm a changed man, blah, blah, blah. Told them my plans for when I get out and what I accomplished while being here. You know laying shit on them nice and thick. My bunky, before he got to this piece of shit on some fucked up charges, was in law school on his way to becoming a lawyer. He helped me write it, so it was sounding real good. Anyhow, I'm hoping that they can let me out early and just give me the rest of my time on parole."

"Do you think that they will?"

"I haven't gotten into trouble since I've been here. Except for when I first got here, and I had to beat this nigga up for trying me. I've attended every last program they have offered so I don't see why not. I'm real cool with the warden, if you catch my drift. Hopefully, she doesn't fuck me over."

Senaj couldn't help himself and laughed so hard it caused everyone in the visiting area, including the guards to turn their heads. For the remainder of the visit, they bullshitted around and caught up with shit they couldn't talk about over the phone. Before Senaj left, he offered up a prayer for his brother in hopes that the parole board let him out on early release. They said their good byes and Senaj dreaded taking his ride all the way home alone. He wished that he was taking his brother with him.

As he made it back to Brooklyn, he had his phone turned off so that he could clear his mind. He prayed damn near all the way back to Brooklyn. He missed his brother tremendously and he wanted to be able to spend time with him before he took on a job. The sun had already gone down by the time he had gotten home and all he wanted was to take a shower and get something to eat. Before going inside of his apartment, he made a call to Rasheed.

"Aye what's up, fool?" Rasheed said, speaking loudly into the phone.

"Nothing much, just getting back from seeing Akuchi."

"Oh yeah? How's he doing?"

"He's doing alright due to his circumstances. He's going in front of the parole board Monday to see if he could get out on early release."

"Man, I can't wait for that fool to get out," Rasheed said, with a chuckle. He looked up to Akuchi as an older brother. His only brother was never around, due to him getting addicted to the glass dick, so Rasheed never bothered.

"Me neither. What y'all fools up to?" Senaj asked, finally getting out of his car.

"I'm just leaving the youth center. All the kids were asking about you. How you just gonna leave them hanging like that? They told me to tell you forget you."

Senaj chuckled while fumbling with his keys. He knew the kids that he grew to love at the youth center didn't mean any harm. Although Rasheed was right about leaving them hanging, he made a mental note to make sure to go check up on them the following day.

"Ahh man, them kids just miss me that's all. I'm gonna check them tomorrow and I'm going to be back in their good graces."

"You could think that if you want to."

Senaj stuck his key inside his door and the strong scent of food being cooked hit him and turned his stomach into excitement. He couldn't wait to get some food in his stomach. He heard Rasheed rambling on about him and Polite coming over and them three playing Call of Duty, as he leaned against the wall next to the door.

"Yo, Senaj, you heard?" Rasheed asked.

"Yeah, my bad. I heard you. Bring some food while y'all at it," Senaj said and shook his feeling off, until he heard his chair in the kitchen slide across the floor.

Rasheed continued to ramble on as Senaj made his way slowly to the kitchen. Once getting to the doorway he peeked his head through the doorway. He was expecting a burglar but what he saw, he was grateful for. He hung the phone up in the middle of Rasheed ranting about some chick with stink pussy and continued to watch the sight in front of him. Senaj didn't know how she kept doing it, but was glad that she did.

Reign was bent over checking on some steak that she thought she would surprise him with. She didn't hear him come in or him being on the phone, due to the headphones she had in her ears. She was hoping to surprise him once he got home. She closed the oven door and once she turned around to sit back at the table, the surprise was on her. She jumped so hard at the sight of Senaj watching her that she might as well have been a cat in a cartoon and sunk her claws into the ceiling.

Reign snatched the headphones from her ears and said, "Dammit, Senaj, you have got to stop sneaking up on me like that."

Senaj smiled, walked up to Reign and pulled her into a tight hug. He placed his lips on hers and cupped her ass in the palms of his hands.

"This is the second time you are breaking and entering

into my apartment, and you have yet to tell me how you are doing this. I know you aren't climbing walls like Spider-Man. Or are you?" Senaj asked, with a raised eyebrow.

"Maybe another time. You're just lucky that I asked if you were going to be home. How was your visit with your brother?"

They took a seat at the kitchen table, he grabbed her leg and put it on his lap and began to massage her foot.

"It went well. He's going to be going to the parole board on Monday to see if he could get out on early release. He wants to do his last five years on parole."

"I hope that he does get out. From what you told me, it's been what, ten years since he's been gone?"

"Yes, I know my parents would be happy. Speaking of, I have to give them a call."

"Well, go ahead. Dinner won't be done for another half hour," Reign said, scooting to her seat and placed her hand on his cheek.

"I'll do that tomorrow before I head over to the youth center. Rasheed been telling me that the kids down there miss me."

"I'm sure that they understand that you are busy."

"Of course, they do. They are still kids though and when they get attached, boy, they get attached. Most of them are coming from broken homes. When they experience love, they want it constantly. I sometimes feel fucked up that I can't be there all the time," Senaj said, with a look of defeat on his face.

"It will be less hectic once you graduate."

"I hope so. I'm going to go take a shower," Senaj said.

He placed a kiss on her lips and made his way to the bathroom. Senaj walked to his bedroom to grab his towel and disrobed. Wrapping the towel around his waist he continued onto the bathroom, and once he set the water temperature to his liking, he stepped in. He didn't realize how tense he was until he felt the stress leave from his body, as the scalding hot water beat down on his body.

Ten minutes later, and he was fresh and done showering. Grabbing the towel, once again wrapping it around his waist, he made his way to his room.

A smile spread across his face as he saw that Reign had placed a pair of clean boxers, basketball shorts, and socks on his bed. His slippers sat on the floor in front of his bed and the clothes that he had just taken off was inside of the dirty clothes hamper. Happier than a kid in a candy store, he rushed to get dressed so that he could have dinner with Reign.

Finally dressed, he made his way down the hallway and noticed that the lights going towards the kitchen were off. There was an illumination bouncing off the walls and he knew that she had lit some candles. Once he entered the kitchen, his mouth could have literally hit the ground. Reign had set the table with their food, several candles around the room and she was standing by her chair. She had swooped her hair into a ponytail, her chocolate skin was draped in a red lace bra, matching lace thong, garter belt, and she wore red fishnet knee highs with red pumps. Gold eye shadow was placed on her eye lids, while her lips were a bright red, begging for him to come kiss them.

"Damn," Senaj said, in a whisper.

With a slight smirk, she asked, "You like?"

"Hell yeah, I do." Senaj began to walk up to Reign but she held her hand up, causing him to stop in his steps.

"Stay right there." Her voice dripped sexiness. She slowly made her way towards Senaj, and once she made it to him, she rubbed her fingers across his bare chest and stared intensely at him. Grabbing his hand, she led him to his chair. Senaj couldn't say anything if he wanted to, he let her take control.

Once Reign made sure that he was seated comfortably,

she stood next to him, leaned over and began to cut his steak up in square pieces and when she was done, she slid in the space between the table and him. Placing a piece of steak on his fork she turned back towards him and fed it to him. She felt his dick pressing against her pussy, making it hard for her to not only concentrate, but also not slip his dick right through the side of her panties and place just the head onto her throbbing clit.

"Tell me, Reign. How do you always manage to sneak your ass in my apartment?" Senaj asked. He honestly wanted to know.

Reign pressed her lips against his and said, "There's so much that I want to tell you and open up to you about, but being that I'm just getting to know you, I can't tell you much. You see, I laid my heart on the line once before and I was hurt tremendously."

"I understand. Trust me I do. But Ma, sometimes you can't just assume or expect for every guy that you meet is like him."

"Look at you trying to sound hood calling me Ma and shit," Reign giggled. Anything to try to divert the conversation to where she knew it was heading.

"Don't get it twisted, Reign. Just 'cause I speak proper English and I'm in my final stage of med school, doesn't mean I'm not hood. I was born and raised in Red Hook and before I made my way to college, I did my fair share of running the streets. Nice try in trying to change the subject," Senaj said, looking directly into Reign's eyes. He reached around her and grabbed his glass, taking a sip of his wine.

Reign, realizing her mouth was open, closed it and thought about what she was going to say. Senaj kept her on her toes, which is why she liked him.

She said, "You speaking proper English has nothing to do with anything. You're right, I did try to change the subject. I'm not really good at this. It's been quite a few years since I've even entertained the thought of dating someone. But you, Mr. Adeyemi, there is something about you that makes me want to let all my guards down. But my stubbornness won't allow me to do so."

Holding onto Reign's ass, he stood up and placed kisses on her neck. He said, "I'm not asking for much, love, just give me a chance. Not everybody is the same and I want to be the one to show you that. I can definitely tell you that you are worth waiting for and Reign, I'm willing to wait it out for you to knock down your walls."

Reign could only smile and nod her head in agreement. She, surprising herself, was digging the shit out of Senaj and while she was scared to, she vowed to try to let him in and not cause him to suffer from Josiah causing her to close her heart.

Senaj laid Reign on the table and rubbed her stomach, staring her down. He didn't understand how God could place a beautiful but broken person in his life. His dick bricked up just from the sight and feel of her skin.

"I need a favor from you," Senaj said, as he placed a kiss on her stomach.

"What's that?" She barely was able to say. Her breathing was shallow because just his kisses alone did something to her.

Senaj tugged at her panties to get them down. He said, "While I'm eating you, I want you to tell me the reasons why you like me."

"Huh?" she said, raising her head from the table.

"You think you could handle that?" Senaj asked, placing his lips on her second set of lips.

"Yes, I can," she whispered.

Senaj used his index and middle finger to spread her pussy lips and moved the length of his tongue across her clit. Her body stiffened, and her eyes rolled to the back of her head. She couldn't even manage to speak, let alone continuously tell him why she liked him.

"You can begin," he whispered.

"I-I like you because you-you're very attractive," she stammered.

"Umhm," he mumbled against her.

"I like your drive. Oh my God!"

"Continue."

"I like that you care about me. You're gonna make me cum, Senaj. Don't stop."

Senaj smiled against her love box. Her pussy dripped goodness, as his face slipped around her juices. His face was coated, and he couldn't help but to lick his lips.

"What else?" he asked.

"I like that you will wait for me. Even though I'm a beautiful nightmare to most. I'm cumming, Senaj." Reign moved her hips in circles as she felt her orgasm building up.

Senaj flicked his tongue rapidly, enjoying Reign's hands pushing his head closer into her. Her moans drove him crazy as his dick was at its hardest. Reign's body shook, as she squirted all over the place. Senaj moved his face, as he rubbed her clit causing her to continuously squirt.

"Please stop," Reign moaned.

"Tell me one more thing why you like me." Senaj growled aggressively.

"I-I-I... Senaj, I can't come anymore!" she yelled.

"One more thing, Reign!" he yelled back.

"I don't like you, motherfucker. I can't help that my feelings developed so fast for you and I'm stuck loving you!" she yelled, as his hand stopped moving and her squirt shot out.

Senaj grabbed her by the neck and roughly kissed her, before going into his shorts to pull out a magnum. Reign did the honors by grabbing the condom from him, she slid off the table, squatted down in front of him, she removed his dick from his shorts and began to stroke him. She placed kisses on the tip of his dick and then slowly glided him into her mouth, as she slowly began to suck, she used her hand to stroke him.

Senaj threw his head back and placed his hand on the back of her head. With ease, she slid him down her throat and made a popping sound when she pulled him out. She looked up at him, making eye contact with him, as she tore the condom package open. His dick bounced in front of her face as she carefully placed the condom on him. When she was done, he pulled her up and roughly put her back on the table, catching her legs in the crooks of his arms. As he glided himself in her, he made sure they made eye contact, causing sparks to fly that they both indeed felt.

***

Two and a half hours later, they lay in bed catching their breaths. They had been all over the apartment leaving a trail of juices along the way. They were silent for the better of ten minutes, until Senaj began to speak.

"What did you mean by you being a beautiful nightmare to most?" he asked, rubbing her arm that was thrown over his waist.

"I had a feeling you would ask. But a small portion of me only hoped that you didn't."

"Is it bad?"

Sighing, Reign said, "It's just something that I didn't want to reveal to you so soon. It may cause you to run from me and that is something that I couldn't deal with right now."

With everything in him, he dropped the subject, as he just kissed her forehead and laid his head back onto the pillows. He got lost in his thoughts, but was abruptly interrupted as Reign shook him. His phone was ringing in her palm. It was an unknown number and he dreaded to answer, but being always on call, he did so anyway.

"Hello," he answered."

"Mr. Senaj?" a tiny voice questioned.

"Speaking. Who is this?" he answered, sitting straight up.

"This is Briana, from the youth center. You said that if there was ever an emergency to give you a call."

"Yes, I did. What's wrong?"

"I'm scared. My mother's boyfriend has been touching me in places he's not supposed to. My mother is at work and he left to go to the store. Please Mr. Senaj, can you help me?" she cried.

"Yes, of course. I will be there momentarily. If he comes back and he does it again then call the cops."

"I can't. He won't let me near a phone. Just please hurry."

With that, the phone hung up and Senaj jumped out of the bed and threw his clothes on. Reign didn't ask any questions, as she followed suit. Senaj called Rasheed and told him what was going on. Rasheed agreed to meet him there.

"Let me drive," Reign said.

Without a thought, Senaj threw her the keys and gave her directions. Like a bat out of hell, Reign flew through the Brooklyn streets as if she was a NASCAR driver. Rasheed was already there once they reached there. They proceeded to the building and took the elevator up to the fourth floor.

"This may be the wrong time to do this, but Reign, this is my best friend Rasheed, Rasheed, this is Reign."

Causing laughter to erupt between the trio, they shook hands and when the elevator opened, things got serious again. They exited and all they heard was a small voice begging for someone to stop. They walked to the apartment marked 4C and banged on the door, causing the other side of the door to get quiet. Footsteps moved towards the door and then stopped.

"Who is it?" Came a rough voice.

"Sir, could you open the door for a minute so that I could talk to you?" Senaj asked, through the door, trying to be patient. His heart pounded in his chest. All he wanted to do at that moment was get Briana away from that monster.

"What for?" he asked.

"I know it might be late, but I just got back from a business trip and I believe that I have a piece of mail that belongs to you. It says confidential and I figured that it may be important."

The guy on the other end of the door hesitated, but soon enough the locks started to come undone. The door cracked just a little bit and Reign's foot went crashing into the door, shocking both Senaj and Rasheed. Briana's mother's boyfriend went crashing to the floor and Reign was standing over him with a gun trained right between his eyes. He was so scared, that piss soaked the front of his pants.

"Go get her!" Reign called over her shoulder.

Rasheed proceeded to call out Briana's name. They found her in a bedroom by the front door. She was naked from the waist down and had her knees pulled to her chest. Her pants were thrown in the far-left corner of the room, so Rasheed brought them to her, as Senaj tried to comfort her.

"You like preying on little girl's?" Reign yelled.

Both Rasheed and Senaj were wondering what the hell was going on.

"No, I don't know what you're talking about?" He yelled, then there was a cracking sound.

"Come on bro, before your crazy girlfriend get us locked up," Rasheed said.

"Briana, did he penetrate you? Or did he just touch you?" Senaj asked.

"He gave me a drink that I thought was juice. It had a funny taste, but I drunk it anyway because I was thirsty. He only touched me."

"Do you have a family member that we could call?" Rasheed said.

"My aunt lives in the next building, on the first floor." she said, with her eye lids drooping.

"Fuck! He must have drugged her. I need you to put your pants on for me, Briana. We're going to get you some help. Rasheed, when she's done, help me carry her to the living room and then go get her aunt." Senaj passed Briana her pants and they stepped out of the room to give her some privacy.

"Why you ain't never tell me that Shorty was about that life?" Rasheed asked, with excitement in his eyes.

"Bruh, I didn't even know. Shit, I'm still surprised about that shit that happened at the door."

"I'm done. Please, I need to sit down. My head is spinning," Briana said.

They entered the room and carried her to the living room and sat her on the couch. Rasheed ran out of the apartment. Senaj began looking for stuff to give Briana to make her throw up. The only thing that he could find was milk. He rushed over to Briana and knelt down in front of her.

"Briana, look, I need for you to drink this. And as bad as I know you probably don't want to, I need you to force yourself to throw up," Senaj said, close to begging her.

"I don't know if I can."

"You have to try, Briana."

Briana forced herself to sit up straight onto the couch, she sluggishly grasped the cup in her hand and forced herself to drink the milk.

"He drugged her?" Reign asked.

"Yes," Senaj answered.

Fire danced in Reign's eyes. There was nothing in this world that she hated the most and that was a pedophile. She had special plans for this nigga and vowed that he would get everything that he was about to get. She would first hand see to it.

Senaj grabbed the empty cup and brought it back into the kitchen. Coming back, he had the trash can. He coached her to stick her finger down her throat to make her throw up.

"Briana!" a woman shrieked.

Both Reign and Senaj turned toward where the voice came from. Briana threw up in the trash can, while Rasheed brought Briana's aunt up to speed. Rage filled Briana's aunt as she made her way over to her sister's boyfriend and kicked him in the balls. Making her way towards her niece, Reign let her know that she needed to get her to a hospital as soon as possible.

"There is only one thing though. You can't mention to the police that we were here. Your niece called you and you came right over. Do you understand?" Reign asked.

"Yes, but what about him?"

"Don't worry about it. He'll be handled accordingly. Take her to your house and call for an ambulance from there."

Senaj and Rasheed sat back as they watched Reign take over. Briana and her aunt left the apartment and left just the four of them. Reign wanted to pull the trigger so bad, but by the look on Senaj's face, she already knew that she would have some explaining to do.

"Can you two gentlemen please excuse me?" Reign asked, politely smiling.

Both of the guys took a moment before they reluctantly left Reign alone. They walked down to Senaj's car not believing what just happened. Only God knew what was about to happen once they were gone.

Five minutes after they leaned against the car, two SUVs barreled down the street and screeched to a stop in front of the building. Senaj and Rasheed looked at each other and shook their heads. Looking at the scene that played out before them, Rasheed and Senaj could only wonder what the hell was going on. As they watched, several men dressed in black climbed out of the SUV's, Rasheed turned to Senaj with his hand opened, ready to dap him up. Looking from the scene to each other and shook their heads.

"Aye bro, I don't know what kind of Shorty you got, but be careful. Shorty seem cool, but she's got a few screws loose," Rasheed said, while dapping Senaj up. He didn't want any parts with what's about to go down and he hoped that his boy took the hint and followed his lead.

"I'll call you in the morning." Was what came out of Senaj's mouth.

He knew he should have followed Rasheed's lead and left, but he didn't know if he would want to know. Senaj watched as Rasheed walk away until he saw movement in his peripheral. He turned his attention towards it. He caught some bulky looking guys throwing something inside the back of one of the trucks. Reign came out of the building and her attention immediately went to Senaj.

She was hoping that he was gone by the time she left from doing her dirty work. But no, there he stood fine as hell, with his arms folded across his chest and his jaw tight. She dismissed her clean-up crew and made her way over to him. Reign knew eventually this was going to happen, but she hoped for more time.

Taking her gloves off her hands, she stood in front of Senaj as if she was a little girl who was about to be scolded by her father. Her hair blew in the crisp November morning air as she looked up at Senaj.

"I can explain," she said.

"That's a major fact. All this shit that's going on and you have-."

*Frrrrrrrraaaakkkkk!*

Automatic machine guns went off around them and both Senaj and Reign's hearts dropped to their asses.

Not long after they had taken cover, Reign's gun was in her hand and her clean-up crew was busting back. Reign looked at Senaj, who had been crouched down watching everything. She grabbed his face in her hands. Her lips touched his.

"I love you, Senaj," she said, once she pulled away from him.

Before he could stop her, she ran out in the middle of gun fire busting her guns, while she made it to her crew.

"Noooooo!" Senaj yelled out for Reign, but the sound of gunshots stopped him. He closed his eyes and pounded his fists against the concrete, causing his knuckles to instantly bleed. He just knew that this would be the last time that he would see Reign.

## Chapter – Eleven
## Pearl

$P$earl had been walking around on egg shells for the past week and a half. After the beat down that Stanley handed to her, she didn't know if she was coming or going. She hadn't spoken to her best friend in a very long time and to be quite honest she didn't know how to. They didn't even get together for Thanksgiving and being that they were so close, they never missed a holiday together.

Pearl hated the fact that she spent Thanksgiving with Stanley and his family. Her bruises were still fresh, and her body ached something awful. To make matters worse, his mother had her help cook and clean, just to have fifty kids running around the house messing things up. Pearl had been trapped in the house since the night of Thanksgiving and she needed to get out of the house.

"Baby." Stanley called from the living room. She stood at the kitchen window and rolled her eyes. Pearl moved away from the window and made her way to the living room.

"Yes," She answered, folding her arms across her chest.

"I need you to run to the supermarket for dinner." He spoke, never taking his eyes from off of the TV.

"There is some food in the freezer," Pearl said.

"Is there steak in the freezer?" He replied, finally taking his attention from the TV.

"No."

"Well, that's what I want you to cook."

"And where do you suppose I go to get steak at this time of night?" After all it was going on nine o' clock and most supermarkets were closed.

"Path-Mark, duh," Stanley said, chuckling.

"That's all the way in Red Hook, Stanley," Pearl whined.

The beer that Stanley was drinking went crashing into the wall next to where Pearl was standing. She jumped as he leapt from the couch and his hand was wrapped around her throat. Her eyes bulged from her head, as she clawed at his hands so that she could get some air into her lungs.

"That's not what I asked you. Take this money and take your ass to Red Hook and get me a damn steak to eat," Stanley seethed.

After glaring at her deadly for a few more seconds, he let her go and she dropped to her knees, gasping for air. Stanley walked away from Pearl and sat back on the couch. Her eyes stung, as tears threatened to fall from her eyes. Getting up from the floor, Pearl made her way into the foyer to grab her keys, sending the deadliest glare that she could, at Stanley. She grabbed her coat and made her way to her car, preparing herself to go on this long journey to Red Hook for some damn steak.

Humiliation was felt throughout her body after she had been riding around for almost an hour trying to find some steak. Stanley failed to mention that the Path-Mark in Red Hook was closed, along with most of the locations. She ended up finding a Fairway that was closing late and she made a bee line to the supermarket.

While inside, she grabbed whatever other ingredients she knew that he liked to go with the steak and checked out. As she got back in the car, she banged on the steering wheel letting out a blood curdling scream that could have busted her windows. Something had to give and soon. Doing what she always did, she pulled up her big girls' panties and decided to deal with it. Finally, making it home, she saw another car in the driveway, which meant that he had one of his friends there.

Shaking her head, she got out of the car and flew inside of the house. Since he was no longer in the living room, she moved her way about the kitchen, making sure that the steak was seasoned to his liking. Setting the oven, she made her way to her room to get out of her clothes. Only to get a shock of a lifetime.

Stanley was laying on his back while a woman straddled his face, rocking back and forth. Pearls mouth dropped, and her breath caught in her throat. The two didn't realize that she was standing there watching everything unfold. Hurt never registered in her, rage was what surfaced. Pearl's hands opened and closed as she turned on her heels and walked down the hallway to the guest bedroom. She rarely went in there, but what she kept in there was well needed for this occasion. Going into the closet, she grabbed the metal baseball bat. As a child she played baseball and had a mean swing. She may have been a little rusty, but she was more than ready to practice.

Pearl crept back into the room and they were now in a more comfortable position with her riding him. Pearl moved closer without making a sound and cocked the bat over her shoulder. Swinging with all her might, she aimed for the girl's body, knocking the wind out of her. She watched as she fell over like a bag of dirty laundry. Stanley just laid on the bed as if he was anticipating this.

"You got a lot of nerve, fucking some bitch in my bed!" Pearl yelled.

"It took you long enough to get back. Is my steak in the oven?"

Flabbergasted, Pearl had to dig in her ears to make sure that she was hearing him correctly.

She said, "You in here fucking another bitch and all you worried about is if your food is being cooked? How dare you have the nerve?"

Stanley sat up and looked over the side of the bed looking down at the chick he was fucking. "Well, I hope you made enough for three to eat."

Anger rose in her chest as she charged at the bed and

swung the bat. She missed by a hair because Stanley moved, but tripped over the girl's body. Pearl ran around the bed, raised the bat above her head, and hit Stanley as hard as she could. The bat connected to his knee causing it to shatter. He screamed out in pain. In a blind rage, she swung again smashing the girl's head, instantly killing her.

"I've told you once before that you got me fucked up! I don't know why I waited this long to do this shit!" Pearl yelled.

She moved closer to Stanley, backing him in the corner. She missed something the first time when she saw this chick on top of Stanley, but as she looked down moving towards him, she instantly wanted to throw up.

Stanley took advantage of that moment and leapt to take the bat out of Pearl's hand. Miscalculating his movements, he realized that he fucked up. He stumbled due to his shattered knee and landed on top of the girl and gaining another whack from the bat. This time to his back, that damn near paralyzed him.

"This chick got a dick! You nasty motherfucker!" Pearl screamed, swinging the bat with every word she spoke.

It hit her that he wasn't eating pussy, he was sucking dick. Pearl beat him until he was inches away from death. Her hair stuck to the nape of her neck and forehead as the sweat poured from her body. She was at her breaking point and she'd had enough.

Snapping out of her daze, her mouth hung open as her heart pounded hard in her chest. Blood was everywhere, and it turned her bedroom into a scene straight from a horror movie. At this moment, she realized that she needed her friend more than anything. She was afraid that someone had heard the commotion and would call the police. She tried not to panic, but it was hard due to the circumstances.

It was time for her to call her best friend. She had done a world of damage and she knew that her best friend or her uncle would be able to help her. The cordless phone was on the side of the bed that she was sitting on. Dialing Reign's number, she kept her eye on both of them, just in case if they moved.

"Hello," Reign answered.

"Hey girl, it's me," Pearl answered.

"Pearl? Oh my God! Girl, you finally got some air from the studio," Reign giggled.

"Studio? Reign, what are you talking about? I got dropped before I was able to sign the contract," Pearl asked, confused.

"What? Every time I would call your cell or the house, Stanley would tell me that you were at the studio or getting rest from being in the studio so much."

Pearl's eyes stung with tears. She was thinking that she had been ignoring Reign for her own selfish reasons and Stanley was the one who was in the middle of everything. Reign asked Pearl over and over again what was wrong, but Pearl full out cried like a big ass baby, snot bubbles and all. After a while, Reign stopped asking what was wrong and just let her get it all out.

"I'm so sorry, Reign. I will explain everything in due time. I need a huge favor from you." She managed to say between the hiccup cry that she was doing.

"I'm on my way," Reign said.

Pearl knew that she would come through and when she hung up, she threw the phone on the bed, and for good measure she hit both of them three times each. Blood and brain matter flew all over the room, confirming that they were both gone. Pearl felt like a weight had been lifted off her shoulders and decided to go take a quick shower, change her clothes and sit in the living room to wait for Reign.

\*\*\*

Mimi

## Reign

Reign placed her sneakers on her feet and made her way to her car. She thought about taking her motorcycle but decided against it. She was taking her Uncle's advice and was keeping a low profile. Since he was one of the people she was laying low from. It had been several days since the Asesino Cartel gunned at her. True to his word, Uncle James was right about them coming after her, but she didn't care. She didn't have anything to lose and she would fight to the end, until death consumed her, or they waved a white flag to surrender.

She had yet to see Senaj since that same night, nor had she spoken to him. He called non-stop and as bad as she wanted to answer, she knew that she couldn't. His voicemails were enough for her at the moment. She didn't want him in the middle of a war that she started. From that point on, she vowed that she would make sure that he was protected at all times. Part of the reason as to why she didn't want to answer his calls was because she didn't want to have to explain anything to him. At least not now anyway, she couldn't risk losing him.

Reign made her way to Pearl with her thoughts swimming. From the beginning, she didn't like Stanley, so for her to find out that he'd been lying about her best friend's whereabouts, for surely once she pulled up, there would be hell to pay.

Pulling into Pearl's driveway, she was glad to see Stanley's car there. That would mean that she would be able to deal with him right then and there.

She got out of her car and made her way to the front door, all the while cursing Stanley out under her breath. She used her key to go inside, Pearl met her at the entryway of the living room picking at her nails. The look in Pearl's eyes was a mixture of emotions. Reign was confused as she tried to decipher by look alone, what her best friend was going through.

"Pearl? Is everything okay?" Reign asked.

"Girl, no! I've fucked up, but there's no one to blame but myself. I'm so mad that in such short time, I let this nigga take full control over my damn life." Pearl expressed painfully, with tears in her eyes.

"Start from the beginning. Where is his punk ass at anyway?"

"Dead," Pearl said, sinking into the couch. Her hands covered her face.

Reign's eyes bulged from her head and she said, "What do you mean he's dead, Pearl?"

"Exactly what I said," she answered. She proceeded to explain to Reign from the beginning about how the abuse began and eventually to how bad it had gotten.

Reign couldn't believe it only because when it had started, she had seen Pearl and didn't suspect a thing.

"That's what the fuck he get. If they're dead, then where are they?"

"Still upstairs. That's why I called you. I figured you would know what to do. So that's why I called you."

"How could you be so sure that I could help you?"

Pearl looked up at Reign and rolled her eyes. It caused Reign to give Pearl the same look, but Pearl responded, "A few months before I met Stanley, I slept with your uncle. His pillow talk was about you. Of course, he didn't say your name, but I don't think he realized exactly how long we had been friends. I think he expects me to believe that he's got more than one niece."

"What did he say?"

"At first, his talks would be more like admiration. Then they began to turn dark and I stopped fucking with him. I never thought he was serious. Maybe he was a little jealous that you were out here doing your thing and getting to the bag. I never thought he meant any harm about it. That was until one night, while I was with Stanley in bed, he had texted me and asked me if I wanted to help him set you up. He offered me twenty thousand dollars to do so. I never mentioned this to you because I didn't want you to do anything crazy to your only relative. That's only how I knew you would help me."

*'Did anybody know about loyalty now-a-days?'* Reign asked herself.

Of course, she was furious with Pearl because if she didn't trust anybody, she trusted her best friend. Reign then realized that she couldn't be entirely too mad at Pearl. If she was any other bitch out here, they would have taken that money and ran. And if Reign knew her Uncle like she thought she knew him, the bitch who did accept the twenty thousand dollars, would have lost her life behind it. James was a greedy bastard and wouldn't stand the fact that somebody was spending his money beside himself.

"While I'm pissed that you didn't tell me about this, you are my best friend and if you need my help, then I will help you. But please, whether you feel like a person is serious or not and they are talking about me, then you need to tell me," Reign said, taking her phone out of her pocket. Searching her contacts for her clean-up crew, she had something in store for her uncle and he wouldn't see it coming.

***

## Senaj

Focusing on his studies had gotten hard for Senaj and he needed to focus more so now than ever. Reign completely disappearing on him took a toll on him and he didn't want to admit it to anyone. Although they hadn't spent much time together, he knew in his heart that he loved her. He wanted to spend more time with her to know her inside and out and make her his everything. He knew she was his everything. Senaj called her day and night, only to get sent to voice mail and it ate him up.

Most days he would get through in a zombie like state. Other days he was hopeful and had an extra pep in his step. If he had to admit to anyone he would have to be honest and admit that he missed the shit out of Reign.

"Yo, Senaj? You've been staring off into space for the past ten minutes," Polite said. They were at Senaj's place, supposedly playing cards, but all that took place was them drinking a case of beer and taking turns with playing Call of Duty.

"I'm cool," Senaj simply replied.

Rasheed raised his lip, only because he knew exactly why he was in a funky mood. After all, he was there the night shit went down. Senaj, once he made it home that night, called Rasheed telling him what went down after he had left. That was a mistake on Senaj's part, because Rasheed wasn't letting it go. The only one who was out of the loop was Polite. He had caught the look on Rasheed's face.

Polite put the XBOX controller on the coffee table and said, "One of y'all niggas want to tell me what's going on? I'm feeling kind of left out of the loop. And last time I checked, we were all best friends."

Rasheed frowned and said, "Your boy over there found out some shit about his girl."

"Like what?" Polite asked, taking a swig from his beer.

"Y'all can just drop it. I don't want to talk about it."

"His girl is some type of killer or something of another," Rasheed said.

"What?" Polite asked, surprised.

"I don't know that for sure, Rasheed. Don't say that until I get the facts."

"My nigga, you told me what happened after I left.

That's enough to be convinced that she is. That girl ain't call you since that night, so that only confirms that what I'm saying is true. I'm sorry, but that chick is in some deep shit, bruh. She doesn't want you to find anything out," Rasheed said, while sipping his beer.

Senaj shook his head and sighed. He didn't want to have to have this conversation with Rasheed and Polite, especially when he hadn't had this conversation with Reign.

"Come on, Rasheed. Don't be so hard on him. A lot of people hold secrets and it's not his fault that his girl got some hidden," Polite said, coming to Senaj's defense.

Shocking both Senaj and Rasheed, because Polite is usually the childish one of the group. Nobody could ever imagine Polite being the sensible one in the trio.

"When did you start making sense?" Rasheed asked.

"I've always made sense. But you two motherfuckers never wanted to listen to me. We are only getting older and it's time we start acting as if we are. Senaj said so himself that he hasn't spoken to her yet, so why jump the gun and start pointing fingers? Especially towards a person that none of us know. Except for Senaj."

Senaj shook his head and sat back on the couch. The point that Polite had made was the point that he was trying to make for the past couple of days. The room was silent until Polite picked the controller back up and began to play the game again.

"You know what, Polite? You're right and I don't know what the fuck I was thinking. I deeply apologize for my allegations and I will keep my mouth shut until you tell me otherwise," Rasheed spoke, with sincerity.

Senaj looked at Rasheed to try to detect bullshit. Not holding it in any longer, Senaj bust out in laughter.

"You had me until you said that you were going to keep your mouth shut," Senaj said, trying to catch his breath.

"Man, I was serious. You so dead set on trying to prove

106

that your girl is innocent to all the wrong people. You know deep inside what I'm saying is true. But that's neither here nor there. So, I'm going to leave that alone," Rasheed said, and swallowed the last bit of his beer.

Senaj continued to laugh and attempted to keep Reign from his thoughts for the remainder of the night. It was all good and dandy until Polite and Rasheed left for the evening. He laid in his bed and while the TV was on, he wasn't paying it any mind. His phone was in his hand and he was looking at the pictures that him and Reign had taken. He missed the simplest things about her, like her smile, her soft snores, and the way she would move her hair over her shoulder when it would get in the way.

"Reign, baby, I miss you. I need you to answer my calls. Or even send me a text letting me know that you are okay," Senaj said out loud.

He felt his heart breaking with every moment that he didn't speak to her. He plugged his phone to the charger and with one last look at the picture, he kissed it and then placed his phone onto his nightstand. He needed to find his girl and fast.

# Mimi

## Chapter - Twelve
### Reign

Reign sat back in her car, waiting for Pearl to come outside. Briefly her thoughts went to Senaj and her heart melted. She had wanted to reach out, but there were things that she wanted to take care of before she did. She looked to her right, checking to see if Pearl had decided to waltz out the door.

Reign rolled her eyes and honked the horn, ten minutes later Pearl exited through the door. She got inside of the car, not realizing the pissed off expression on Reign's face. She laughed once she caught it.

"Girl, what you looking at me like that for?" Pearl asked.

"What the fuck you took forever and a day for? Just to put on some jeans and sneakers?" Reign asked, now annoyed.

Pulling her car onto the street she made her way to her Uncle James house. She hadn't seen him since she gave him his money from the last hit she did on Jose. He hadn't made an attempt to call her, but she didn't either. She figured that being that she was considering getting out of the game soon, she needed to square things away with him. Reign and Pearl made small talk while going to Uncle James house. Reign purposely didn't tell Pearl where they were going. Only because, she didn't want Pearl to back out when she questioned her uncle about him going to Pearl to set her up.

Once Pearl realized where they were, she asked, "What are we doing here?"

"I haven't seen my uncle in weeks. I'm gonna be going away in a few months and I want to make sure that we are on good terms," Reign responded, with a smile.

Although Pearl didn't believe her, she got out of the car anyway. The wind was blowing something vicious and the skies looked as if there was a storm brewing. They pulled their coats closer to their bodies to shield themselves from the cold. Reign's phone made a dinging sound, alerting her of a text message. It was from Senaj. It read:

*Bae: Reign, you ignoring me is not cool. It's been almost three weeks since I've seen or spoken to you. If you are doing this because of that night, just know that I'm not here to judge you. Nor am I wanting an explanation. I miss you like hell, Reign, and this is the most painful shit that I've been through in a long time. Baby, please just pick up the phone to call me or text me to let me know that you are okay. This may not be the right way to say this to you, but girl, I love you. Please reach out to me.*

That message alone made Reign teary eyed. Slipping her phone back into her coat pocket, she didn't bother to respond. She had a task ahead of her and she wanted to make sure that she was on point. Pearl and Reign walked up the stairs to the front door. Reign took her keys out, tried to open the door, but her keys didn't work.

She and Pearl glanced at each other as she tried once more to open the door, again it didn't unlock. All her sense went out of the window as she began to beat on the door. Uncle James was home, so she didn't know why he was taking so long to answer.

After Reign banged on the door for ten minutes, James finally came to the door. His face was turned up and didn't look very happy to see Reign. His eyes bulged widely as he noticed Pearl with Reign. He wore the surprise well on his face.

"You gonna let us in, Unc?" Reign asked, with a smirk on her face.

"Sure. What brings you by? I haven't seen you in a while," Uncle James said before turning his back to the two girls and walking towards the living room. They walked in after him closing the door behind themselves.

"Well, I've taken your advice on staying low after doing

the hit on Jose. Apparently, somebody is after me."

"I told you that they would be. You did an anonymous hit without making sure what the background information was, and you done got yourself in a world of trouble. You didn't want to believe me. Reign, your head is so far stuck up your ass, you don't take heed it somebody trying to help you out," Uncle James said. He walked over to his bar and poured him a glass of Crown Royal Vanilla.

"You know what I find very amusing, Uncle James?" Reign asked.

"What's that?"

"The fact that you could sit there and tell me some shit like that, when you have been trying to set me up for the longest. And you did so thinking that I wouldn't find out."

"Set you up? That's absurd! You're my niece for crying out loud."

"And obviously that doesn't mean shit to you! I know all about you trying to have me killed when I did that run for you. I know all about when you tried to have my best friend set me up, only the fact that you didn't know that she has been my best friend for years!" Reign said, jumping in Uncle James face.

His face dropped once he realized that the cat was out of the bag and she knew everything.

"So,what you gonna do, Reign? Kill me right here where I stand?" he asked, spreading his arms with a sly smirk on his face.

Reign returned the same smile that he'd given her and said, "Oh no. That would be too easy. You can join the hunt right along with everybody else. Just know that I expect for you and only you to try to come after me. And just because I know where you lay your head won't be an advantage for me. I'd give you the benefit of the doubt and trust that you will keep it in the streets. Since after all, you let several people in the street know that we have beef. Until I see you again and it's til the death."

Reign raised her hand and pointed her two fingers towards him as if she was holding a gun. She smiled and acted like she was shooting him.

A lump formed in his throat, as he looked on from Reign to Pearl. His love for money is what got him into this predicament and he knew he couldn't win against her. Although he had killed before, he wasn't a trained killer like Reign was. She could kill with her bare hands. James watched as Reign and Pearl backed out of his house.

"Did it really have to come down to that, Reign? You're gonna kill him over what?" Pearl asked, as they made their way to Reign's car.

"Yes, it did."

"Over what?"

Reign stopped walking and turned to Pearl. Her cheeks were wet with tears and her eyes were blood shot red. "What do you mean over what? His disloyalty to not only me, but to my father as well! Instead of protecting me and making sure that I was good, his greed for money is going to get him killed!"

Pearl wanted to cry with her friend. She had never seen her cry, so she knew that her friend was beyond hurt. Pearl wanted to grab Reign into a hug, but she just let it be for right now. They climbed inside of Reign's car and drove around the streets in silence.

To say that Reign was hurt was beyond the truth. She was more devastated than anything. She hated that it had to come to this. When they pulled up to Pearl's house, she waited for her to get out.

"Reign, I can't imagine what is running through your head right now. I know beginning this war with your uncle is not what you should do. He is your family," Pearl said. In her mind she thought that she was trying to make things better. That was far from what she was doing.

Reign turned her head to Pearl and shook her head. "I don't see him as my uncle any more. He is now my enemy. Nothing that you say is going to make that change. He's going to get what's coming to him, period."

Pearl didn't bother to answer Reign. She would never see where Reign was coming from because she wasn't as street wise as Reign. Pearl climbed out of the car and went inside of her house. Reign sped off, leaving tire marks and smoke. Her mind was made up and it all went out of the window when Jameson told Reign James' plan.

For hours on end, Reign drove around crying her eyes out. How could family treat you so wrong after you done them so right? James' money mostly came from Reign putting in work. She basically fed, clothed him, and kept a roof over his head due to all the hits she's done. Reign couldn't believe his disloyalty.

The sun was down by the time she pulled up in front of Senaj's apartment. She looked up and saw that his light was on. All she planned to do was go up for a few minutes to lay in his bed to get his scent. She realized she needed more than that and decided to just face the music, sooner rather than later. Sighing, she turned the car off and climbed out and made her way upstairs. She paused in front of the door open.

Pausing at the sight of Reign while she was still beautiful, Senaj automatically knew there was something wrong. He moved in closer to her and placed a kiss on her forehead, down to her nose, and to her lips. His arms wrapped her as he pulled her inside. The tears began to flow again as he lifted her from her feet and placed kisses on her lips, until she opened her mouth to receive his tongue.

Walking them into his room, he laid her on the bed and got her undressed, doing himself next as he spread her legs open. He slid inside of her raw and moved in her slowly. He missed her something crazy and at that moment, he just wanted to feel her on him.

Reign grabbed Senaj by the back of his head and moved her hips to his rhythm, all the while with tears cascading down her face. She no longer cried for the situation with her uncle. She now cried because she knew soon, she couldn't possibly be around Senaj and risk losing him or putting him in harm's way.

Senaj long stroked Reign and moved close to her ear and said, "Don't you ever fucking leave my ass without an explanation. I deserve that much from you even if you feel like I don't. I put my heart on the line with falling for you, Reign. This shit wasn't planned at all. Do you understand?"

Always becoming putty in his hands, she became submissive. She moaned, "Yes, Senaj, I get it and I apologize deeply. There is just so much shit that I've been dealing with on my own."

"You don't have to tell me right now, but you need to clue me in afterward," Senaj said, as he lifted her leg up in the air.

Her finger nails clawed into his back as he dug in her deep. Senaj placed kisses onto her chest, onto her breast, making a circle around her nipple. Her back arched and her body shook as she came all over his dick. Senaj, however, wasn't done. He pulled himself out, flipping Reign into doggy style. Senaj almost came prematurely because when she got into position her arch was so perfect. Her ass was tooted up just right and her pink pussy was peeking from the back screaming for Senaj to enter her.

Senaj grabbed the base of his dick and grabbed her ass cheek with his free hand. Her pussy farted, causing both of them to laugh. His dick throbbed as his blood pumped into his member. He slipped the head of his dick over her clit causing the right amount of juices to cascade all over his dick. His eyes closed as he entered her again and he felt her pussy tighten around his dick.

"Fuck!" Senaj exclaimed.

Reign didn't give him time to compose himself as she began to throw it back on him. This was exactly what she needed to release her stress and she was going to make it count. Senaj raised his hand and sent a stinging blow to her right cheek causing her to yelp. He dug deep inside of her, hit her spot, and made it feel like he was touching her stomach.

"Oh my God, baby! Yes, right there!" Reign screamed out. Probably having his neighbors wondering if he was killing her instead of her pussy.

"Right there, Ma! That's your spot! Whose pussy is this?"

"You know it's yours. All yours, Senaj." Beads of sweat formed on Reign's forehead as she worked up her second nut.

Grabbing her ass cheeks, Senaj spread her ass cheeks and watched as his dick went in and out of her, coating his dick in cream. Before he was ready to cum, Senaj turned Reign onto her side and lifted her leg onto his shoulder and climbed in between her legs and placed him inside her again. Her mouth dropped in a perfect "O" as he instantly hit her spot.

"I know you ready to cum again, so you might as well and cum with me, Ma." Senaj grunted. He had been ready to explode, but he didn't want to so early.

Reign's moans escalated 'cause she was no longer able to speak. They both felt each other's body shake and while Senaj grabbed one of her breasts in his hand and the other went around her neck. Senaj drove into her, feeling his nut ready to come out.

"Oh shit! Oh shit!" Reign said, with each stroke.

"Oh shit, babe! I'm 'bout to cum all over your ass!"

And literally he pulled himself out and jerked himself off until his thick cum landed on her ass cheeks, in her crack, and her hair. His body jerked as she managed to turn in just the nick of time to catch the last little bit of his nut in her mouth, sucking to make sure that she had gotten everything. Senaj removed himself from her mouth and fell out on the bed. They both laid next to each other without exchanging words, trying to cool down and catch their breath. Reign laid with her eyes closed because she knew what was about to happen.

Surprisingly, Senaj was quiet for a good fifteen minutes, laying with his eyes closed.

Raising her head up onto the palm of her hand, Reign looked at Senaj and said, "Are you hungry? I could make you `something to eat real quick."

He opened one eye and said, "Yeah, I could eat. Make sure you make you something to eat, too."

"I will," she said.

As she got up, Senaj smacked her on her ass, causing her to look over shoulder and smile at him. She grabbed one of his t-shirts and put it on. She pranced out of the room and headed to the kitchen to make them something to eat. She found some thawing chicken wings inside of the fridge and decided to make them fried chicken wings, mashed potatoes, and string beans. Keeping herself busy in the kitchen she didn't have the time to think about Senaj confronting her. The food was almost done when she felt his presence behind him. His chocolate skin glistened under the lighting causing his skin to look like he was oiled up. Reign couldn't help but to cast her eyes across his body. His muscles were ripped, and she was tempted to touch.

"What you over there looking at?" Senaj asked, smiling, showing his chipped tooth.

"My man," Reign said, looking at his print through his boxer briefs.

"Oh, your man?"

"Yep. I put ownership on that," Reign said, walking

116

closer to Senaj.

"Don't start something that you're gonna have a hard time finishing. I have weeks of buildup, baby girl," Senaj said, with a chuckle.

"And you think I wouldn't be able to keep up? You must not know me, darling," she said, wagging her finger in his face.

"Over the three weeks that you've been MIA, I asked myself that question over and over again."

Reign, being that he didn't say what he said loud enough, thought she incorrectly heard him. She knew nothing was wrong with her ears though, so she knew that she heard him right. She paused in her steps to the stove and turned around towards him.

She said, "What did you just say?"

"I said, I asked myself that same question over the last few weeks," Senaj retorted. Granted this wasn't a good time to have an attitude, but he felt like he had every right to. He wouldn't get anything off his chest or find out what was really up if he kept letting her sweep it under the rug. Like what he witnessed was something he saw every day. For crying out loud, he didn't know if he had lost her. Thanks to his technology, the only reason he knew she was alive was because even if she didn't respond, the message would tell him that she read it.

"Are you serious? You gonna do this right now?" Reign spoke. She couldn't believe him. They were having a good night and of course she didn't want to have to get into this with him at the moment.

"Reign, if we don't do it now, then when will be the time to do it? When you decide to want to disappear again?" Senaj asked, taking a seat at the table.

"It's harder to just come out and explain it to you, if I'm still trying to deal with things."

"If you could just call me your man, then you should be

able to tell me anything. Doesn't matter how hard it is for you to get it off your chest. I've went three weeks without speaking to you. Not a phone call nor a text and you just show up like I'm not gonna want to know answers."

Reign stood at the stove taking the rest of the chicken out of the pot and placed them on a pan covered in napkins to drain the oil. Her head ached, and she just wanted to lay down. "Senaj, you can't possibly think that it's that easy."

"Actually, I do think that it's that easy. You're just the one who is making it hard. As sure as your mouth can open up to debate me about this for the last few minutes, the same thing you could have done to explain to me why you've been MIA. Oh, and what the fuck happened at Briana's house? Are you a killer? Are you apart of some mob? These are things I have to know, Reign. I'm going to be a doctor soon. Don't you think that it would be important if you weren't being so selfish?" Senaj was furious.

"Wow! I'm being selfish Senaj? You're the one who keeps asking for an explanation, when you texted and said that you didn't need one!"

"Because I figured you would be woman enough to tell me!" Senaj slammed his hands onto the table and stood up. His nostrils flared as he looked down at her. He didn't want it to be this way, but he knew being civilized wouldn't get him anywhere.

Reign pulled her hair behind her ears and licked her lips. She folded her arms across her chest and said, "First of all, I'm gonna need for you to tone it down quite a few notches. I don't know why you think that I owe you an explanation. Yes, I do get where you coming from, but you should be able to respect the fact that I'm even considering telling you anything."

"Respect?" Senaj snorted.

"Yes, I said respect. You know what... I don't want to do this with you. I came over here 'cause I did miss you. I didn't go about things the right way but still in all, I made it to you. Could I have went about it another way? Sure. Should you be sitting here yelling at me like I'm your child? Absolutely not. We are adults for Christ's sake, Senaj. I get the tension. I understand how you feel but baby, please just give me some time. Without jumping down my throat about it."

Senaj unfolded his arms from his chest and closed the distance between them. He looked at her intently in her eyes and moved his hand to her face. He kissed her lips, pressing hard down on them.

He pulled back and said, "Obviously you don't care that I have my career on the line for the mess that you've caused. I don't need my name coming up in anything that had to do with that night. If you can't understand that, then I'm not sure what's going to happen."

With that being said, Senaj left her mouth hanging open, as he turned on his heels and walked back to his room. Reign leaned against the counter as she took in the words that he said. Surely, she didn't want them to end over something that she could possibly prevent. Her heart was heavy, and it was battling it out with her mind. Although her mind said just to forget it and cut ties with him, she knew better than that.

Finishing up the food that she was making, she took a seat at the table, she did something she hadn't done in a long time. She prayed. She prayed for forgiveness for all the killings that she had done, she prayed that Senaj would find it in his heart to forgive for anything that she had done wrong, and she prayed for God to give her a sign that it would be okay. At the moment she said amen, there was a picture that had fallen off of the wall. She smiled as she shook her head and picked it up. It was time for her to face the music. She walked to Senaj's room and opened the door.

"Babe, can you come into the kitchen, so I could talk

with you please?" Reign asked, walking up to his bed, holding her hand out for him to grab.

Placing his book onto the bed, he took her hand and said, "Sure."

They walked hand in hand into the kitchen, where Reign had set the table. They took a seat and Reign began. She said, "I didn't want this turn out this way. I'm sorry for saying the things that I said, and I would really like for you to forgive me. Before you say anything, all I ask is that you hear me out. I'm not good at this, because I've never done this. Just bear with me. Can you give me that much?"

"Yes, I can," Senaj said, before picking up his fork and placing string beans into his mouth.

Sighing, Reign began, "I am a hired killer. Assassin, if you will. I have been since my father passed, he was the one who trained me, and I picked up where he left off. The other night at Briana's house, that was the Asesino Cartel coming after me. My uncle told me that they would be after me, but I didn't think that it would be this soon."

"Why are they after you?" Senaj asked, trying to digest what she had just said.

"About two months ago, before I met you, I walked inside of a McDonald's. I ordered my food and took a seat. Normally, I don't eat in public places because of the line of work that I am in. In the corner of the restaurant, there was a woman who was balling her eyes out. I mean she was crying to the point where her eyes were so puffy, she could barely see out of them. Once again, normally I don't speak to people in public either. There was something in me that told me to talk to her. Maybe there was something that I could do to help. She began to tell me that she had recently found out that her daughter was pregnant at only seventeen. The thing that really broke her heart was the fact that the child's father was her man." Reign spoke, looking at Senaj with a can-you-believe-this look.

"She told me that she found out that they had been fucking with each other behind her back since her daughter had been fourteen. Her daughter had two abortions before she had gotten pregnant recently and she didn't know what to do. So, I did what I only knew how to do. I let her know that I would be able to help her, but it would cost her. She told me that she didn't care, that all she wanted to do was have this nigga pay. I don't take to kindly to niggas taking advantage of young girls, so that only fueled my fire even more. I only charged her twenty thousand and promised her that he would get taken care of." Reign looked up at Senaj to make sure that he was following her. He nodded his head, indicating that he was. Reign continued with her story.

"Being that I didn't get that case from my uncle, I walked into it blindly and didn't know that he was a part of the cartel. Unfortunately, I found out from my uncle and he told me about the time my father had a run in with them. He warned me that they wouldn't stop at anything until they were sure that I was dead. Especially, because of who my father was, and they despised him. I didn't expect for them to come after me so soon. I wanted to be able to have time to get things in order so that I wouldn't have to look over my shoulder. My plan was to take them down one by one until they decided to wave a white flag of surrender."

Senaj inhaled deeply. He hadn't expected her to say all of that. He didn't know what to say and was rendered speechless. All he could say was, "Wow."

"On top of all that, I found out that my uncle has been trying to have me set up for the longest. I confronted him tonight and it was bad. We are now at a war because of his disloyalty."

"Why do you think he tried to set you up?" Senaj asked, biting into a piece of chicken.

"He found out that my dad left me close to seven million dollars and he was trying to go after it. I don't know how he thought that he could, because I just found out that bit of information. I don't even know where the fucking money is at. Everything is going so wrong in my life, Senaj and you are the only thing that is going good. I want to make sure that you don't get hurt. I'm sorry, I should have let you know sooner, but you have to believe me that the less people that know, the better."

Reaching across the table, Senaj grabbed her hand and said, "Listen, you were this way before me. There is absolutely nothing that I could do to change that. Do I like it? No, because there are so many things that can happen to you and I don't know how many times I could express, I would lose my mind if something was to happen to you."

"I don't need you to do anything, Senaj. I got this handled. Just continue to worry about your studies to become the best doctor that you could be. I promise that this won't affect you in any way. I will make sure of it," Reign said.

She got up from her seat and walked over to him and placed a kiss on his lips. Although Senaj was skeptical, he slightly believed that it was true. And he would believe it until he saw otherwise.

# Chapter - Thirteen
## Senaj

"See! I told you. But don't nobody ever want to listen to my ass!" Rasheed said.

Senaj was on break at the hospital and he had called his friends on three way. It had been a full week since Reign came clean, and he needed to get it off his chest. He hated to admit it to them, for the simple fact that Rasheed would throw it in his face. He rolled his eyes as he played with a piece of paper that was on the table in front of him.

"Bruh. This is not what I need right now. I just couldn't keep it to myself. I don't know what to do," Senaj admitted.

"What do you mean you don't know what to do? You are about to become a doctor. That should be enough for you to know what it is that you should do. You can't possibly continue to be with her," Polite responded.

"Let me ask y'all a question," Senaj said, sitting up straight.

"What's up?" both Polite and Rasheed answered.

"Y'all ever been in love?" he asked seriously.

The phone went silent, before Rasheed bust out laughing. In the background Senaj heard Polite say, "Oh, my God."

He didn't know why he tried to confide in them. He knew that they were both childish and couldn't be serious.

"You can't be telling me what I think you telling me," Polite said.

All the while Rasheed hadn't stopped laughing.

"Yes, I am," Senaj spoke, standing firm.

"This nigga!" Rasheed howled.

In a hushed but serious tone, Senaj said, "Can y'all be fucking serious for a quick minute? I'm tired of you two acting so fucking childish when it comes to certain shit. You would think because y'all are my best friends you would

123

know how to deal with a serious situation. Yes, I love Reign. I'm not so sure what to do because of it. All I'm asking is for advice, not y'all's critique. Stop acting like middle school boys and be fucking real with me."

The phone line went silent, as Rasheed and Polite took in what he said. They knew they had finally struck a nerve with him and decided to put shit aside, the joking, just so that they could be there for him.

Polite spoke first, "Senaj, man. We didn't know that you were that serious about her. Our fault, man."

"Well, I am. So, what should I do?" Senaj asked, placing his chin inside his hand.

For the better part of Senaj's lunch his best friends gave him different scenarios about what it is that he should do. Nothing they said, he thought would work. He thought about just dealing with it one day at a time. So far that's all he would be able to do. Hanging up the phone, he proceeded to walk out of the break room, but three beefy Spanish looking guys pushed him back inside. He looked at each one of them, engraving their faces into his brain.

"What can I do for you fellas?" Senaj asked, placing his hands inside of his lab coat.

The smaller, in height, guy walked to the front of them and said, "Actually you can. Would you mind telling us where Reign is at?"

"Reign?" Senaj asked, trying to prolong the question so he could come up with a good lie.

"Yes, Reign," he said smugly.

"Well, I did watch the news this morning and they did say that there would be a slight chance of rain," Senaj said, with a slight smirk and chuckle.

He wasn't prepared for the punch that was delivered to his gut. He bent slightly over, as the wind was knocked out of him.

"Now. Let's try this again. Next time don't be a wise

guy. If you do, all of your doctor friends will have to do everything they can to save your life," The guy whispered inside of his ear. He placed a gun right under his rib cage.

"I don't know who you're talking about," Senaj said, finally standing straight up. He had a look on his face that would kill.

"Well, people say otherwise. They've said that they have seen you with her."

"Well, wherever you are hearing it from, they are feeding you false information. I don't have the time to entertain anyone. As you can see, I'm doing my residency."

The guy smirked and folded his hands across the top of his protruding belly. He said, "You know, I can't quite believe you nor them, I have yet to see it for myself. But I will say this, if I happen to see you with her, around her, or even walking past her, there will not only be there hell for her, but for you as well. Just because you lied. So, you better be careful. I'd hate it if an innocent person got in the way of something that had absolutely nothing to do with them."

Senaj's jaw tightened. This was exactly what he didn't want to happen. But he knew the risks and he would have to deal with it. He nodded his head, letting the men know that he understood. They left just as fast as they entered. Senaj, with fury, punched the locker that was behind the door. He took his phone out and texted Reign and let her know that they needed to talk and fast. He told her to come down to the hospital as soon as she could.

*** 

**Reign**

"Pearl, would you like to go out for dinner? I'm starving. It feels like I haven't eaten in weeks," Reign said.

They had been laying around Pearl's house all day

trying to figure out Reign's next move. Pearl came out of the kitchen with two cups filled with strawberry banana Henny colada's and fancy straws.

"Hell yeah. I feel like I could eat a horse right now." Pearl laughed.

Reign side eyed her and said, "Bitch, you look like you can. Not for nothing, you look like you gained some weight. You pregnant?"

"Girl, don't put that over my life. Hell no. Thank God."

"Have you taken a pregnancy test?"

"No."

"So, how you know? You know I want a niece or nephew. I don't have any siblings and you're the closest thing that I have as a sister." Reign whined.

"Bitch, have one yourself then."

Raising her hand, Reign said, "Umm, no. No chance in hell. I have too much going on right now to be thinking about having any kids. Plus, when I come out of hiding, I'm gonna put in some work."

"What if Senaj wants you to have his baby?" Pearl asked.

Reign took a sip from her drink and responded, "We haven't spoken about that."

"But what if y'all do and he wants you to have his child?"

"I haven't thought that far. We'll cross that bridge when we cross it."

Scooting up in her seat, Pearl said, "Okay, how about this question? Would you have his baby?"

"How did this turn to me?" Reign laughed.

"Because it did. Now answer."

"So demanding. Like I said, I haven't thought that-"
*Blacka! Blacka! Blacka!*

Shots rang out and glass shattered as Pearl and Reign ducked for cover. Bullets hit the sofas and pillows causing all the feathers and cushions to fly around the room. Reign took the gun from the small of her back and blindly shot back. Pearl was crouched down behind the dining room table, praying that a bullet didn't find its way to her.

The shots ceased and after a few minutes, Reign came from her hiding spot and ran to the door to look out.

She stopped mid run, as she saw her uncle's car sitting there idling. The passenger window was down, and he sat leaning across into the passenger seat to make sure that she saw him. The message rang clear for Reign as she raised her hand to fire back, but he sped off just as the first bullet left the chamber.

"Fuck!" Reign yelled, just as Pearl came out next to her.

"What just happened?" she asked, with feathers all in her hair.

"I'm going to need for you to find another spot to stay at. I will pay for it no matter the cost!"

"Reign -"

Reign looked at Pearl and yelled, "This is not up for debate! That was James and I will not have you caught up in this! Just like I won't have Senaj caught up in it! Find a hotel and I will pay for it until you find another spot. Get you some shit together and go now!"

Pearl saw the seriousness in Reigns eyes. She ran back in the house and with lighting speed, she packed two suitcases in less than eight minutes. She threw them down the stairs and dragged them to her car. When she was done, she found Reign who was standing in the middle of the madness inside of the living room, looking at her phone. Her face was screwed up and confused.

"What's up?" Pearl asked, out of breath.

"Senaj said he needs me to go down to the hospital. He needs to talk to me."

"About what?"

"He didn't disclose that in the text. Here take my credit

card and book a room. When you get settled, text me and let me know where you staying, and the room number. I'm going to go see what Senaj want to talk to me about."

"Okay. I got you. Be careful, Reign. If you see James, put a bullet in him for me, for fucking my shit up," she said with a hug.

They walked out of the house together getting into their separate cars. Reign went one way and Pearl went the other way. Reign couldn't wait until she caught her uncle. He asked for nothing, but trouble and Reign was going to give it to him. Reign made it to Mount Sinai Kraivs Children's Hospital in no time. She parked and exhaled, before she walked into the emergency area looking for Senaj. She texted him to let him know that she was there.

Five minutes later he came out with stress written all over his forehead. They kissed, before he took her by the hand and led her into one of the rooms that wasn't being used.

"What's up, baby? What was so urgent?" she asked, making eye contact.

"Three dudes just left here not long ago. They were looking for you," he said, dragging his hand across his chin.

Reign's breath caught in her throat. This is exactly what she feared. She asked, "What did they look like?"

"Spanish. Two of them were tall and one short. They were stocky ass men."

"What did they say?"

"They asked me if I knew you and then threatened that if they saw me with you, passing you, or even around you that I would be a casualty to the war basically. Reign, what have you gotten me into?"

Reign's mouth dropped, and she thought about her words before she decided to say anything. She couldn't be mad at the words that he chose, because he was right. She did something before she met him and the cause of it was putting him into danger.

She said, "Senaj, I apologize to you sincerely from the bottom of my heart. The last thing that I want to do is put you in harm's way. But please allow me to fix this situation."

Senaj was confused. He just wanted to be able to live out his dream and not die before he actually made it come true. His heart was telling him one thing and his mind was saying another. If he wasn't so deeply in love with her, his judgment wouldn't be so clouded.

"What can I do to help?" he asked, instead of saying what he really wanted to say. Which was, *'This can't work.'* But he didn't, he wouldn't dare.

"Nothing. Let me handle this. I promise I got it."

"Are you sure?"

"Yes, I'm positive."

Senaj pulled her into a hug and kissed her forehead. He said, "I know you were spending time with Pearl because of all of the lost time y'all had, I'm sorry for pulling you away from her."

Reign shook her head and said, "I had to put her up in a hotel. My punk ass uncle came and shot her shit up."

"What? Are you serious?" Senaj asked. He backed up and looked Reign over to make sure that she was okay.

"I'm fine, babe. I'm gonna deal with him, too."

"You know that this is a test for our relationship, right? I can only be honest with you and I need to tell you what my thoughts have been lately. So many times, recently I told myself that I had to end things with you. I can't bring myself to do so, Reign. No matter this crazy situation," Senaj said, honestly.

"I know, babe, and I appreciate you sticking around. Trust me I would have been left me if the shoe was on the other foot," Reign admitted, while laughing.

"We'll get through this. One last kiss before I have to go back to work," Senaj said.

He bent down and placed his lips on hers. After their kiss, they departed and made plans to meet up again as soon as Senaj was free from the hospital.

\*\*\*

## Pearl

Sitting on the bed inside of her hotel room, she ran her hands through her hair. She didn't know what the fuck was going on and why she had to be thrown in the middle of it. Granted, she loved her best friend but being down to ride was something that she had to think about. She didn't know if she was qualified to help her friend bust any guns. Pulling out her cell phone she texted Reign, letting her know that she was situated and decided to take a shower. Being that the room was on Reign, she decided on room service as well.

After her shower, she sat on the bed in her robe and rubbed her stomach. Before Reign asked her if she was pregnant, she had taken a pregnancy test and it came back positive. She wanted to tell her, but she wasn't so sure if she wanted to keep the baby. After all its father was her abuser and he was now dead. Her biggest fear was to take care of a baby on her own and she was suddenly facing her fear.

Turning the TV on, the news immediately came on. The reporter was standing in front of a warehouse wrapped in layers of clothes. She said, "This is Marcy Godiva and I'm reporting live from an old abandoned warehouse off Nelson Street in Red Hook. Reportedly there was a disposed body found by a local resident. The identity of the body is unknown at this point. Now reports from the NYPD are stating that the head had been beaten in badly and there could possibly be no way of being identified. More on this story at eleven. I'm Marcy Godiva, reporting live. Back to you at the station."

Pearl's heart dropped to her chest. She knew that this was Stanley coming back to haunt her from the afterlife. Her heart sped up in her chest causing her to panic. There was a knock on the door, but she was scared that it was the police. She muted the TV and listened as the person beat on the door.

"Room Service!" the person on the other end of the door said impatiently.

She crept slowly to the door to look through the peep hole. She was relieved to see that it was room service and not the NYPD. She slowly opened the door, peering at the lady who stood their impatiently.

"I'm sorry I took so long. I was in the shower," Pearl said, as she opened the door wider.

"No worries. Here is your food and enjoy your stay at The Hilton," she said.

"Hold on one second let me give you a tip." Leaving the door open, Pearl went inside her purse and took out a knot of money. She peeled off two twenties and placed them inside of the lady's hand. She closed the door and went to go sit down to enjoy her meal of filet mignon, mashed potatoes, with mushroom gravy and asparagus. She also ordered a slice of red velvet cake and strawberry cheesecake. Before she could dig into her food, there was another knock on the door.

"Coming!" She called out and wrapped the ties on her robe. She saw Reign on the other end as she looked through the peep hole. She opened the door and dragged her inside of the room.

"What is wrong with you?" Reign asked.

"Bitch, they found Stanley's body," Pearl said, shook.

"How do you know that?"

"It was on the news."

Taking a seat on the bed, Reign reached for an

asparagus and said, "You know they find a bunch of dead bodies every day."

Sighing, Pearl took a seat next to Reign. She asked, "Do you know where your crew dump his and that tranny's body?"

"Actually, I don't know. I just tell them to dispose them and they do as I say."

"But as an assassin, don't you need to know where the body is for just in case purposes?"

"Pearl, you're being too paranoid. They did not find his body. Did they say his name?"

"Well, no."

"Okay. Then you have nothing to worry about. Listen, my team is efficient. I can assure you that it's not Stanley."

"Okay. But once they say otherwise and they mention his name, I need the first flight out of this country." Pearl laughed but was very serious.

"Okay, I got you."

Reign had decided to stay the night at the hotel with Pearl. She knew her friend was shaken up about what happened, and she wanted her to know that she wouldn't ever leave her out in the storm. The next day she planned on hunting out the guys who had confronted Senaj.

Pearl went to bed with thoughts of her unborn child in mind and she had committed on keeping it and raising it alone. She knew she would have her best friend to help along the way.

## Chapter – Fourteen
## Reign

The rain was pouring down as if it was spring time instead of it being the dead of winter. Christmas was approaching, and Reign looked forward to the gift exchanges between her and Senaj. This was the first Christmas that she would enjoy in a long time. It was two thirty-two in the morning and Reign had been sitting out front of an old one-story family home out in the suburbs of Long Island. She found out where the small guy that had visited Senaj stayed and planned on dealing with him.

The house was quiet as everyone had fallen asleep. That was until there was a light that came on. She used her night vision binoculars and looked towards the house. She hoped it wasn't one of his kids getting a drink from the kitchen, but then she saw that it was him, scratching his ass and standing in the fridge, letting his dick swing.

Placing her binoculars on the passenger seat, she picked up her AS Val and balanced it on her shoulder so that it was pointed right at him. She looked through the scoped and once her target was made, she pulled the trigger and dropped him with one bullet. The only noise was the glass shattering and the screech of tires, as she got the hell out of dodge. Her next stop for the night was to the club that was owned by the head nigga in charge. She was prepared to send him a message that she knew would leave a lasting impression. Driving into the SoHo section of Manhattan, she noticed that there was a small crowd out front of the salsa club. At that moment, she didn't care how many people were standing outside, she didn't care that innocent people would be harmed. All she wanted to do was to send a message letting Pablo know that she was ready for war.

Standing across the street in an alley, she hoisted the grenade launcher onto her shoulder and trained it onto her target. She prepared herself for the kick back and let off two. They instantly erupted on contact. People screamed as Reign walked away to her car, not looking over her shoulder.

The next day it was all over the news what happened at the salsa club and guaranteed it made Pablo pissed. He ordered to every one of his henchmen that if they were to see Reign to not kill her, but to bring her to him. He wanted to be the one to end her life. Little did Pablo know, that she had a team that was a force to be reckon with. They had precise orders to kill as many of his henchmen as they could and then she would come out of hiding to deal with Pablo.

The morning of Christmas, Senaj woke Reign up to some Christmas head. Head so good that he had her shaking for the remainder of the morning. He had the day planned out and a surprise for her that he couldn't believe himself. He made her breakfast fit for a queen and sat her at the dining room table.

"I just want to thank you for putting everything that you have on hold in order to spend Christmas with me. This has by far been the best Christmas for me in a long time. I love you Senaj," Reign said, after she had opened the first gift he gave her. It was a pair of black Red Bottom shoes. She hadn't even bought herself a pair, only because she knew how expensive they were. Although she had the money she wouldn't dare buy them.

"It's nothing for me to do to make sure that you are happy. Just you being here in my presence has made me the happiest man in the world."

*Ding! Ding! Ding!*

Reign looked on, confused as to who could be at Senaj's door. She figured that it could be someone after her, so she stopped Senaj from opening the door. Senaj tried to speak but she silenced him by staring at him deadly, daring him to say another word. She reached for her gun that she had hidden behind his sofa cushion.

Senaj knew who was at the door but he enjoyed watching her act a complete nut case with a smirk on his face. Reign reached the door and looked through the peephole, only to notice that it was an elderly man and woman who resembled Senaj. She rushed from the door and back to where Senaj was sitting with his arms folded, a smug look on his face.

"I think it's your parents at the door. Why didn't you tell me that they were coming, Senaj? Oh my God! I have to change," she whispered, then ran to his bedroom.

Senaj chuckled as he made his way to the door to open it for his parents.

"Mom! Dad! Tu me manques!" he said in his native French tongue. It meant he missed them.

"Tu nous manques trop!" Both his mother and father responded. Telling him that they missed him, too.

Senaj invited them in and into the living room. He took their coats and told them to have a seat.

"How was your flight?" he asked.

"It was just fine. Thank you for the tickets, son," his father said.

"Anything for you guys, of course."

"Senaj, where is this girlfriend that you told us so much about?" his mother wondered, looking around the living room.

"She went to go freshen up," he said, chuckling, remembering how scared she looked. His parents looked at him like he was crazy which caused him to abruptly stop laughing.

"Have you spoken to Akuchi?" asked his father.

"I haven't spoken to him since I went to go see him a few months ago. He hasn't reached out through mail or phone," Senaj said, realizing that he had been so wrapped up in Reign that he missed the fact that his brother hadn't contacted him.

"Oh no. I hope that he hasn't done something to get himself in more trouble," his mother said, holding her chest.

"Mom, don't worry yourself. I doubt that he would get himself into any more trouble. Last, when I went to see him, he was going to be going in front of the parole board. He's trying to get out and I'm pretty sure that he's only focusing on that," Senaj said, making his mother feel at ease.

"Wow, elle est belle," said his mother, as she looked beyond Senaj.

Senaj happened to look behind him and had to do a double take. He didn't know how she was able to look so good in such little time. She had changed into a white slim fit body-con dress with the black red bottoms that she had opened. Her hair was in a wet and wavy style and tear drop diamond earrings adorned her ears. She had on silver bangles with a diamond necklace. His mother was right, she was fucking beautiful and he was proud to be able to flaunt her on his arm. He stood up and stood next to her.

He wrapped her in a hug and in her ear, "Fuck are you, a magician?"

She laughed hard and realized that his parents were looking at them. His father's mouth was hanging open and his mother elbowed him in his gut.

Senaj said, "Mom, Dad, this is my girlfriend, Reign. Reign, these are my parents, Akachi and Zain Ademyemi."

"It's a pleasure to finally meet you. I wish Senaj would have told me that you guys were coming. I would have been better prepared," she said, as she took each one into a warm hug.

"Oh no. You're fine. It's a pleasure to finally meet you. All Senaj does is talk about you," his mother said.

"Aww. He's the sweetest," Reign said and placed a kiss on his cheek.

They sat around the living room and made small talk.

Senaj eventually made his way to his room to go and change into some decent clothes. By the time he had gotten back, his mother had dragged Reign into the kitchen to cook. Senaj joined his father in the living room to watch A Christmas Story. Once on commercial, his father turned to him and looked at him seriously.

"Yes, father?" Senaj asked. He already knew where this conversation was going to go.

"Nothing. I just want to tell you that I am very proud of you. You are almost done with completing your dream and I just don't tell you enough how you are making every one of us proud. If your brother didn't get caught up, he would have been doing something with himself."

"Dad, it was self-defense."

"Not in the eyes of the white man. He was a stone-cold killer. Didn't help that the man was an undercover cop. The fact that he was a dirty one, is the only thing that saved him."

"While that is true, they still shouldn't have charged him for all these years."

"A murder is a murder to them, son. The fact that his skin was the color of coal played a major part in that sentencing," his father said, turning up his nose.

"No, dad, I don't think so. I think that it was solely about the fact he had murdered someone."

"You tell that story all you want to. Do you know what happened at the parole board?"

"No, he hasn't contacted me at all. I promise, Dad, when tomorrow comes, I will contact the facility and see what's going on. I just hope he hasn't done nothing to get himself into any trouble."

"One more thing, son."

"And what's that?"

Akachi turned to Senaj and said, "Son, so you really love that girl in there?"

Senaj turned his attention to Reign who was laughing at

something his mother had said. He undoubtedly was in love with Reign. Her smile alone warmed his heart every time he saw it.

He turned back to his father and said, "Yes, dad, I do. It hasn't been long for us, maybe three months tops but she just has this energy that pulls me into her. I'm not saying any time soon, but I see myself marrying her and she will be the mother of my children."

"I believe you. The way that you just looked at her, I could tell that the way that you feel for her is something real. I look at your mother that way. Hell, I've been looking at her since I first met her. You make that woman an honest one. Do you know if she feels the same?"

"You know what I have an idea. She's tells me she loves me, but hasn't really gone into depth."

"Have you met her parents?" he asked.

"No, sir. Her parents passed away when she was younger."

"Oh?"

"Yes. And yes, I know how, but I would rather not speak about it because that is something that she would volunteer. I already told you enough."

"Okay. I can respect that."

For the remainder of the evening they enjoyed each other's company. Senaj liked the fact that Reign blended right in. His parents liked her as well and he knew that he was for sure going to make her his wife someday.

*\*\*\**

### Reign

The next day, Reign and Senaj decided to go out to dinner with Pearl. This was his first time actually meeting Pearl. He hadn't seen her since the first night he had tried to approach Reign. They arrived at The Soul Spot located on Atlantic Ave in Brooklyn. It was a soul food restaurant, that was prided on their dumplings. Pearl was already there waiting, looking nervous. Reign walked up to her and gave her a hug and then introduced them.

"Finally, I get to meet Mr. Man," Pearl said, laughing. She took her coat off and hung it on the back of her chair. Senaj and Reign did the same thing and took their seats.

"Well, blame your best friend from not allowing us to meet," Senaj said, laughing.

"Oh no. You are not blaming me for shit," Reign said, smacking him upside his head.

They took their seats and ordered their drinks. Senaj had a rum and coke, Reign had Sex on The Beach, while Pearl stuck to a Sprite. Reign folded her hands on top of the table and looked at both Senaj and Pearl. A smile spread across her face.

"You okay?" Pearl asked.

"Yeah, why?" Reign asked, still with the smile on her face.

"Because you are sitting there looking like you crazy."

Reign sighed and said, "You act like it's a crime for me to be happy. I'm just glad you two are finally meeting. After all, you both are my favorite people."

Pearl twisted her face up and took a sip from her soda and decided that she would tell Reign the news about the baby.

She began, "Reign, I have something to tell you and I don't know how you will take it."

"There is nothing that you can't tell me that I wouldn't support you," Reign said, grabbing Pearl's hand across the table.

"I'm pretty sure about that. Only because we spoke about it and I know how you feel about what I'm going to tell you."

Reign raised her eyebrow and tried to think about what it was that Pearl could possibly want to tell her. She said,

"What is it?"

"You're going to be an auntie."

"Oh my God! Are you serious? You told me that you weren't, you heifer."

"I know but that was only because I was scared, and I didn't want to raise this baby by myself."

"Oh, shut up. You know as long as I got breath in me, I'm going to help you with anything that you need."

Before they got into their conversation, Senaj managed to slip in a congratulation and for the next ten minutes he was excluded from the conversation. He didn't mind because that was her friend and he knew, no scratch that, he wouldn't even try to get in the way of that. While they spoke Senaj noticed that there was a crowd forming in front of the restaurant. He was trying to see what was going on, but it was too late, because shots rang out. Reign looked towards them and with her eyes and a slight head nod she directed Senaj to get Pearl out of there. Although he was pissed, he did what he knew he had to do. He grabbed Pearl by her hand and they ran out towards the back exit.

Reign ducked down in the booth and tried to see what was going on around the pandemonium. People were running in every direction trying to find an exit. In the midst of everything, Pablo sat in his wheel chair with an AK-47 on his lap. He had five dudes surrounding him and more were walking through the crowd, throwing bodies because they were looking for her.

Lately, she had been caught slipping and she cursed herself She knew that she couldn't be out in the open, yet she still played herself and came out. Her thoughts ran through her mind, as she tried to figure out how she would be able to escape or how she could knock these niggas down one by one.

There was a window of opportunity where she was able to run towards the back. In doing so, Pablo saw her and shot in her direction. She slid behind the buffet style counter and took cover. She peeked her head out and took the opportunity to shoot back. She took down two of his men and ducked back.

"Reign! Come out now and let me just kill you!" he said, with a crazy laugh.

"Fuck you, Pablo!"

"You started this, Reign! If you wouldn't have killed one of mine, this wouldn't be going on right now!" he screamed, sitting in the same spot that he was in when he entered.

"Fuck you once again, Pablo! You want me come get me!" she yelled.

The bullets began as his men shot up the counter. She placed her hands over her head and drew her knees to her chest. Once they stopped, she stood up and raised her two nines and took down three more of his men before they knew what was happening. She went back down and just prayed that she had enough rounds to last her throughout this ordeal. She checked her magazines and tried to think smart. She didn't have many rounds left and she still had quite a few of his people she had to take down.

"I'm gonna kill you just how I imagined killing your father! Too bad his heart took him out before I got the chance to!" Pablo said.

The mention of her father boiled her blood something bad. She knew now that tonight would be the night that Pablo would die.

*** 

## Senaj

Senaj jumped into his car with Pearl and took her home. He despised the fact that he had to leave Reign, but deep down he knew that she could handle herself. He knew that if he tried to stay with her, she would give him hell and they would be arguing about it later on when they saw each other again. Pearl sat quietly, until Senaj had asked her the directions to the hotel that she was staying in. He figured the least he could do would be to take her best friend home.

"What was that about?" Pearl asked.

"I don't know. I don't ask any questions. She tells me to bounce, I bounce," Senaj said.

"Doesn't that make you feel like less of a man?" Pearl asked.

Her face was straight, so when Senaj turned and looked to her, he couldn't tell if she was joking or not.

"What?" he asked.

"I said…"

"No, I heard what you said, but what do you mean? Does what make me feel like less of a man?" he asked, not grasping her question.

"Taking orders from Reign?"

Senaj thought about her question and then laughed. He laughed so hard it put Pearl in her feelings. He said, "Hell nah. Why would it?"

"She's telling you what to do."

"No, I don't know how you interpret that from what just happened. Whenever in a situation like that, and Reign tells me to go, I'm going. I know that she can handle herself and it doesn't bother me that she is putting herself on the line just to make sure that I'm good. Now if the shoe was on the other foot, it would be the same way. Reign was trained to do this shit. So, I know that she is more than capable to deal with it."

Pearl didn't have anything else to say. Senaj just put her in her place and she didn't like it at all.

In the beginning, when Senaj first found out, he did feel a certain way. No, he didn't feel like he was being selfish by not staying back and helping. He didn't know the first thing about guns and he wasn't about to try to figure it out and shoot himself in the process. The rest of the ride to Pearl's hotel was in silence. Soon enough, Senaj had pulled up to the hotel and waited for Pearl to get out.

"Senaj, can you walk me up? Just to make sure that I get up there safely," Pearl asked.

He didn't want to, but reluctantly he got out of the car. They walked inside of the hotel and he followed her to the elevator. The ride, just like in the car was silent. Senaj just wanted to be able to get home to wait for Reign's call and then call it a night. The elevator doors opened up on the 9th floor and they exited.

"Thank you. Please make sure that Reign is okay and tell her to give me a call when she can," Pearl said, with a smile on her face.

"As soon as I speak to her, I got you," he said.

For a few seconds there was an awkward energy. Senaj smirked and went to turn away, but Pearl grabbed him by the arm and in the same movement, she pulled his neck towards her face and tried to plant a kiss on his lips. Senaj's eyes ballooned and he struggled to not make contact.

Finally, after almost a full minute, she let him go. Tears escaped her eyes and she covered her face.

"Pearl, what the hell is wrong with you?" Senaj said, backing up a safe distance away from her."

"I'm sorry, Senaj. I shouldn't have done that," she whimpered.

"You think? What the hell were you thinking?"

"I wasn't. I'm sorry. The way this pregnancy has been having me lately, I've just been tripping. Please, don't tell Reign about this," she said, realizing that there was a possibility that he would.

"What you mean, don't tell Reign? What kind of nigga you think I am? She's my girl. Why wouldn't I tell her? And don't try to blame nothing on you being pregnant. You only been pregnant for two minutes. I don't want to hear that shit." Senaj was pissed. From everything that Reign told him, he had felt bad for her, but at this moment, he didn't care anymore. In his eyes, Pearl wasn't shit now.

"Please Senaj! She won't never forgive me," Pearl cried.

"That's something that you did to yourself. You should know better." Senaj seethed.

"Please."

"Let me get out of here before I decide to get rude," Senaj said. He whipped his hand down his face and walked back towards the elevator. He couldn't believe what just happened.

*'The nerve of this chick blaming it on her pregnancy.'* He thought with disgust.

\*\*\*

## Reign

Within minutes, Reign had taken down all of Pablo's henchmen. It was now time for her to handle Pablo. The comment he made about her father disturbed her. Reign stood up from behind the counter and looked at Pablo who sat so confidently in his wheelchair. He raised his gun, but when he pulled the trigger, the gun jammed.

Reign ran at him full force, screaming loudly. Once close enough, she jumped and using both of her feet, she kicked him square in the chest causing Pablo to fly out of his chair and sent his gun flying. Pablo's face twisted up in agony as Reign collected herself up from the floor and stood over him.

"Oh, you ain't so bad now without your goons nor your gun. Now what was that comment you made about my father?" Reign said, as she squatted over him as if she was in a position to ride him.

"Fuck you! I should have killed him long before that

heart attack!" Pablo said, coughing holding his chest.

Using the palm of her hand she hit Pablo in the nose and his hands shot up to hold it. Blood ran down both of his cheeks.

"You think my father would really let you take him down without a fight? Are you stupid or are you dumb?" Reign stood straight up and kicked him in his ribs. She moved away from him and sat in a chair. Figuring that he wouldn't move anywhere any time soon, she folded her legs.

"My death won't go unnoticed and you will have plenty more people coming after you."

"And I will deal with that when the time come. I was really hoping that this could have been a more exciting kill, but unfortunately it hasn't been. The cops are going to be here soon, and I need to go. But first I must do something." Reign stepped over Pablo once more and pulled his shirt from his pants. Several times Pablo tried to sneak hit her, but she would only deliver blows to his ribs to stop him. She reached down in her boot for her ninja star and began to carve her name into his stomach.

"Arrghhh!" Pablo yelled, and punched Reign on the side of her head.

She rolled from off of him and onto some broken glass. She cut her hands up from the tiny shards and anger arose deep inside of her. She got up from the floor and kicked him on the side of his face sending teeth skidding across the floor. His hands once again flew to his face and she took the opportunity to slam her foot into his face. She managed to break his nose, jaw, and some of his fingers. Reign zoned back in and heard sirens off in the distance. She pulled her gun out and shot him between the eyes. She looked at him with disgust, as her gun smoked.

With only minutes to spare, Reign ran behind the counter in search of a manager's office or anything that could direct her to the security system. She happened upon a small room and inside of the room, Reign found an older woman, huddling under a desk. There were monitors on the wall.

"Where is the tapes?" Reign asked.

The woman looked up at Reign like a deer caught in head lights. Reign didn't have any more time to waste, she pointed the gun to the woman and she started moving like there was fire under her ass. The woman started crying as she waited for the disk to extract. Once it was, she handed it to Reign and Reign once again raised her gun and shot the woman. A bullet straight to the heart.

Reign ran out of the back and into a parking lot, making sure that she stuck to the shadows. Reign hated the fact that she let Senaj drive. She had no way to get her ass out of this situation without being detected.

Reign ran down the block and waltzed up to a dude getting out of his car. He walked up to a mailbox and left his door open. With lighting speed, she ran and hopped inside his car and drove off. She didn't close the door until she was two blocks away. She breathed a sigh of relief once she had gotten fifteen minutes away from the scene. Reign rode around for an hour before she ditched the car a few blocks from Senaj's apartment and walked the rest of the way. Of course, she let herself in.

Reign looked around the apartment in search of Senaj and found him inside of the shower. She got undressed and scared him by joining him. Her hands were bloody and instantly he began to panic. She assured him that she was okay, but he made her get out of the shower. Reign placed the lid down on the toilet and took a seat, while Senaj rummaged through his cabinets to find his first aid kit.

"What the hell happened after I left? Did you get hurt anywhere else? Do you need to go to the hospital?" Senaj asked.

Reign giggled nervously and responded, "I kicked his ass, what do you think? No, I'm not hurt and if I was hurt anywhere else I doubt that I would have to go to the hospital. Remember you're going to be a doctor."

Senaj shook his head, as he used some tweezers to pick out small pieces of glass. He cleaned her hands with some peroxide and then wrapped them up in elastic gauze bandages. He took her by the elbow and placed her back in the shower and made her keep her hands up in the air while he washed her.

Her heart warmed, as she watched him take care of her delicately. She couldn't have asked for anything better than this moment. When he was done with her, he quickly washed himself and helped her back out of the tub. He wrapped a towel around them both and walked into his room. In there, he moisturized their bodies, then gave her just a t-shirt and boxers and he put on some basketball shorts. They laid down in the bed and turned the TV on. The news was on and the story about the restaurant shooting was breaking news.

"I'm glad that you're okay." Senaj mentioned.

At that moment, he tossed around the idea of telling Reign about Pearl trying to come onto him. He decided not to, because he didn't want to come in between their friendship. Deciding not to, Senaj left the room to go heat up some frozen pizza being that they didn't get a chance to eat at the restaurant.

"Babe?" Reign asked, snuggled under Senaj after stuffing themselves like a fat pig.

"Yes," Senaj answered. His eyes were closed, and he was in his happy place.

"Have you heard about how Briana was doing?"

Senaj's eyes opened, as he cleared his throat. That night was a touchy subject for him because of Reign leaving but he couldn't avoid the question.

"I did. Her aunt contacted me a few days after everything happened. She told me that Briana's mother didn't believe anything that she was saying. Said that Briana was lying about the whole thing. It fucked Briana up so bad that she had to go and see a therapist. Her aunt also said that she ended up filing for custody. I won't know how anything else turns out until she contacts me again."

"I hope she does get custody of her. Any mother who could deny the fact that their child, their daughter no less, is being touched by a grown ass man, should not be a parent. There should be a special hell for bitches like that."

"I agree. Come on babe. Let's get some rest," Senaj said, and pulled her closer to him. She turned around and placed a kiss onto his shoulder. They said good night and fell asleep in each other's arms.

## Chapter – Fifteen
## Senaj
## New Year's Eve

"**B**abe, can you please come on! By the time we get there the club is gonna be closed!" Senaj yelled from his living room.

Since the incident, Reign had spent all her time with Senaj. Whenever he wasn't at the hospital, they were together. A few times during that week, Reign had thought about trying to track down that seven million. She thought that it would be a waste of time and figured that it could have been a tactic that her uncle was using in order to trap her. She wasn't hurting for the money and she would not allow greed to consume her, like it had done with her uncle. If it was in fact true, the truth would come to light and she'd have it.

"Here I come! Is Rico and Tony outside?" She yelled back to him.

Rico and Tony were the two security details that she hired after she had killed Pablo. She was tired of being caught slipping. Granted she was cautious, but having some extra eyes was a bonus. She couldn't see everything.

"Yes. I spoke to them and they said they had a few of their people to situate themselves inside of the club. They also told me that you wouldn't have to pay for the extra help because they would pay them," Senaj said.

He had taken it upon himself to walk to the bathroom. His breath was caught in his throat, as he looked Reign up from the bottom of her feet to the top of her head. She was downright beautiful. Reign wore a red body hugging dress. The dress had long sleeves and stopped in the middle of her thighs. She had on black thigh high boots and diamond bracelets adorned her wrists. Her make-up was light, only using a little bit of foundation, gold tinted highlight for her cheeks and gold eye shadow. She had done her hair in beach curls and wore chandelier earrings.

"Why you just standing there looking at me like that?" Reign asked, with a smile showing all of her teeth.

"You standing there looking like a Victoria Secret model and you asking me why I'm looking at you the way I am?" Senaj asked and walked up to her and hugged her from behind. He placed a kiss on her ear and they looked at each other inside of the mirror.

"Me? Have you seen yourself Mr. GQ?" Reign said, giggling and pushing him away with her butt.

Senaj was wearing black True Religion jeans with a dark brown shirt and beef and broccoli Timberland boots. His hair was freshly cut, and his waves was on full display. His goatee was trimmed with perfection and diamond studs was shining in his ears. He ran his hand across his shirt as if he was dusting dirt off of his shirt and posed with his arms across his chest. Reign giggled and pushed him away.

"No, seriously. Is there a way for me to tap that before we leave?" Senaj asked, biting his bottom lip.

"Some of what? This?" Reign asked and smacked her own ass then put her hands on the sink. She bent over just until her nose touched the mirror above the sink and she made her ass cheeks clap.

"That's how you feel?"

"Pretty much," Reign said and winked at him in the mirror. She put some red lipstick on her lips and proceeded to walk out of the bathroom. Senaj grabbed her by the arm, causing her to halt in her steps.

"You can't just tease me like that. You see what you did?" he mentioned. He grabbed her hand and put it over his bulge. His dick was constricted in his pants, wanting to break free.

"Were you not the one who was just rushing me? Now

you want to try and get in a quickie. Not gonna happen but I can guarantee that it's all yours when we get in. Come on, let's go before Rico and Tony think we not going nowhere and they leave." They grabbed their coats and made their way to the stretch limo out front.

The ride into Manhattan was a good one. They put on the radio and listened to Funk Master Flex mix it up, as they drank on champagne, Hennessey, and other kinds of liquor. They arrived at Copacabana on 47th street and stepped out. The line to get in was long, going down the block and almost around the corner. Thank God, Reign had some connections and gotten them into VIP. Senaj took Reign's hand into his, as she wrapped her waist length black mink around her body. At the door, there was a guy getting in the bouncer's face, causing them to delay the process of letting people inside of the club.

"No! I'm not leaving. Why can't I get in?" the guy yelled.

"Sir, you don't have ID," the bouncer said, without so much as raising his voice.

"Well, I'm not leaving until I get in and this party is over! And everybody in this line is going to have to have a heart attack about not getting in, cause I ain't moving!" the dude said, folding his arms across his chest.

"Sir, this is my last time telling you. Please move before I have to move you myself."

"If I got to leave, somebody gotta reimburse me for this Metrocard! I ain't pay six dollars for nothing!" he yelled, causing the people who were in earshot to laugh. Reign and Senaj shook their heads and entered the club by showing the bouncer their VIP passes.

"This some bullshit!" They heard the dude yell as they walked in.

They made it just in time to grab something to eat from the buffet style dinner. They had a little bit of everything and went to go enjoy the open bar and dance floor. Both Senaj and Reign was feeling good and was glad that they had decided to spend New Year's out and not at home. They were having fun dancing and sipping.

Around eleven thirty, Rasheed and Polite had mad it and they were equally having fun. Despite putting their homeboy at risk, they couldn't help but to accept Reign. They knew their boy was in love and couldn't do nothing but to accept that they were going to be together.

"Y'all ready! We got one minute until the ball drop! Grab somebody up for that kiss at midnight," the DJ said. He cut the music and the gigantic screens on the walls displayed the ball dropping from Times Square.

Senaj grabbed up Reign and stood her in front of him. He nibbled on her ear, as they watched the ball drop.

"Ten—nine—two—one. Happy New Year!" the crowd yelled. Reign turned around and placed her hands on Senaj's face. She smiled before she placed her lips on his. Senaj's heart was pounding in his chest with excitement.

"I love you," Reign said, against his lips.

"I love you too," Senaj responded. The music had kicked back on and the dancing resumed. Later that night, as Reign promised, she gave Senaj more than a quickie and might have put a hooker or porn star to shame.

\*\*\*

## Pearl

Pearl was lying in bed, where she had been for the past four days. She had even spent New Year's there. Her doctor had told her to take it easy due to the fact that she was at risk for having a high-risk pregnancy. There was a possibility that the baby wasn't getting enough oxygen. She hated that she had to be bed ridden but there was nothing she could do. She was getting ready to get up to go use the bathroom when her phone started to ring. Grabbing it off the bed, she rushed to the bathroom. It was Reign calling her.

"Girl, you not gonna irk me every day on the hour." She laughed, as she released herself.

"Yes, I will. I'm just making sure that you are okay."

"If I wasn't on bed rest would you be just making sure that I was okay?" she asked.

"Girl, yes. You know that, so stop it."

"Yeah, yeah, yeah. What are you doing?" Pearl asked, while flushing the toilet.

"I'm getting some rest. Girl, I've been hung over since New Year's. Now I see why I don't partake in any turn-ups. My ass is still stuck in bed wishing I had the energy to get out of the bed," Reign said, as she twirled her hair around her finger.

"Where's Senaj?" Pearl asked. She wasn't sure if Senaj had said something. She took it as him not doing so, only because Reign hadn't mentioned it to her.

"He's at the hospital. He's been there for two days already and I miss him."

"What are you going to do when he gets a job in the hospital?" Pearl asked.

"The same thing. It's like that now. I get time to do what I want to do while he's gone. And it gives us time to miss each other."

"Ugh! Y'all irk me," Pearl said, laughing.

Joining in with her laughter, Reign said, "What do you mean?"

"Y'all act like y'all in love or something. It's sickening."

"I wouldn't say that we are in love, but I could definitely tell you that we do love each other. And you know what? It feels good to do so. After Josiah, I didn't want to have anything to do with men. I felt like I was going to make another mistake. I didn't have the time for it. But then in walked that fine as chocolate milk that night at Smalls Jazz club-"

"Girl, you didn't even like him then. What the fuck you talking about? You forget who you were talking to? Like I wasn't there and had to hear about it for the rest of the night."

"You should have known then that it was going to happen. I couldn't shut my mouth about him." Reign laughed.

Pearl laughed so hard she couldn't help herself from snorting while laughing. In between breaths, she said, "Wait. Wait no I have to ask you a serious question. I can't stop laughing."

"Would you come on? I got to go. Senaj isn't letting me skip lunch today. He said I need to get my hungover ass up and bring him lunch," Reign said, laughing.

"Okay. Okay. Have you spoken to your uncle?"

The smile that Reign had on her face faded. Just at the thought of her uncle put her in a distasteful mood. She sat up in the bed and said, "No, and I'd rather cut his head off and create a shrine, then to talk to him."

"Reign, you can't hold this grudge against him."

"Pearl, I will do anything that I want. Did you forget that he shot up your fucking house? Did you forget that he was disloyal? You were there for mostly everything. Down to him trying to set me up and you gonna just tell me that I shouldn't hold a grudge against him! That baby is sucking all of your senses."

"Whoa, whoa, whoa! Hold it there, Charlie. This is definitely not why I asked you. I was just seeing if you came to your senses. No need for you to throw my baby into it."

"Pearl, cut it out. You know damn well I didn't throw the baby in it like I'm talking about him or her. Cut your shit! Furthermore, you should have thought that question through, before you asked me. Uncle or not I'm holding this grudge until I'm holding his head."

Pearl, remembering what her doctor said about taking it easy, sighed. She wasn't about to raise her blood pressure and possibly risk losing her baby. She said, "You know what? I apologize for getting into your business. I shouldn't have asked you and I swear you will hear nothing more out of me about it. I have to go. I got to get something to eat."

With that she hung up the phone and said out loud to herself, "I should have had your boyfriend fuck me."

*\*\*\**

## Reign

Reign walked into the hospital in search of Senaj. She had finally gotten herself together and brought him some lunch. She made seafood stir-fry with Jasmine rice. She packed him an apple juice and a slice of homemade sweet potato pie. By now several nurses knew who she was and while some greeted her, others would look snobbishly over their shoulders. She'd of course dismiss them because she knew that they only did it, because he was the fine young doctor. Even though she was bringing him lunch, she was on a mission. She went through the doors for the emergency room waved at the nurses at the nurse's station and walked towards their usual meeting spot at the coffee machine.

"Hey girl, you look good," Nurse Sasha said, walking past the coffee station.

"Thank you. Have you seen Senaj?" Reign asked, getting to the point.

"Actually, I have. He was rushing to use the bathroom to make sure that he made it here before you did." She giggled. Nurse Sasha was an older nurse, who had been married for almost thirty years. If it had been one of these hot in the ass young nurses who had said that, then she would have been sending their bodies to their parents' house.

"If you happen to see him before he gets here, let him know that I'm waiting," Reign said, with a slight giggle.

"Sure will. And like always it's always nice to see you," Nurse Sasha said, and walked away. When she did, Senaj was walking up with a smile on his face.

"Hey babe, I missed you," Senaj said, leaning over to give Reign a kiss. He was stopped short, due to a swift punch to the gut.

"Hey babe, my ass. I can't believe you." Reign hissed through her teeth. The look on her face could have killed him.

"What are you talking about? And why are you hitting me?" He strained to say.

"You tried to fuck my best friend. I should have known that you was like the rest of these niggas out here. I can't believe that I fell for you." Reign's heart was crushed. The tears begged to drop from her eyes, but she wouldn't allow it.

"What? Reign, what are you talking about?" as soon as he asked that, he knew just where she heard it from.

"You ain't shit just like the rest of them!" she yelled.

"Babe, I didn't try to fuck Pearl. She tried to fuck me, and I stopped it."

"You're lying," she cried.

"I promise you that I'm not. I'm not perfect but I wouldn't do that to you."

Reign shook her head, as much as she wanted to believe him, she couldn't. She experienced this kind of heart ache one too many times that she couldn't.

Senaj saw her heart breaking right in front of him and knew that he had to do something or say something to fix this situation.

He exhaled and began, "Look babe, I would never do nothing to hurt you. I didn't try to fuck Pearl. I would never

156

even try to. The night that everything happened at the restaurant and I drove her back to the hotel. She asked me to walk her up. Once at the door, she tried to pull me in for a kiss and I stopped her."

Something was eating Reign up to believe him, but she just knew she couldn't. She knew that when men get caught in those type of situations they would lie or do just about anything to not lose their girl. Shaking her head one more time, she turned and walked away.

Senaj called out to her and she just kept walking. He watched, as she walked through the double doors possibly out of his life forever. With nothing to punch, he walked into the break room with the food that Reign had brought him. He placed it on the table and shook his head, as he dialed Polite.

"Hey, aren't you supposed to be helping patients right now?" Polite asked, with a chuckle.

"Yes, but I need to talk right now. Are you busy?"

"No, you just caught me getting ready to get to lunch. What's up?"

"Bro, she left me. Her dumb ass friend tried to have sex with me, blamed it on the pregnancy, and then told Reign that I was the one who tried to fuck her."

"What?" Polite yelled.

"She didn't want to believe me. And I could understand why because of the shit she went through her ex but damn she didn't even give me the benefit of the doubt. She took Pearl's story and ran with it."

Polite cleared his throat and whispered, "Aye, I know a couple of females that wouldn't mind doing me a favor. Give me shorty address and I could send them."

"No, she's pregnant, Polite." Senaj sat down, sighing.

"What are you going to do?"

"I don't know. That's why I called you. I can't let her believe this shit. I have to go. I'm going to try and figure something out."

"Good luck, bro. Call me back and let me know how things turn out."

Senaj couldn't believe his luck. He started to walk out of that hospital to go find Pearl and confront her. *'What good use would that do? Reign's probably on her way over there now to confront her. Me going, would only make me look guilty like I was trying to hide something. Nah, I'm good. The truth will come to light.'* He thought to himself and continued to do his job.

The pain she felt was all too familiar. Remembering how she felt, when she had caught Josiah in her bed with another female came crashing on her heart. She was barely able to make it out of the hospital without blacking out. She had become so dizzy that she had started to see black spots and had to lean against the building as soon as she made it through the sliding doors.

*'Mommy and Daddy, I'd give anything to have y'all right now. I don't know if I could deal with this heartache alone,'* she said to herself, as she climbed into her car. Before she put the car in park, she sat there for a few and tried to slow her breathing. She didn't want to hyperventilate too much, and something happened while she was behind the wheel.

Reign took her phone out of her pocket and wanted to text Senaj so bad but once she saw that he didn't send her one, even to apologize, she said fuck it. She started her car and made her way towards the hotel. She knew that there were always three sides to a story, his story, Pearl's story, and then the truth. She was about to get ready to find out the truth.

Breezing past the people that was in the lobby, Reign made her way upstairs to Pearl's room. Using her own room key, she opened the door and let herself in. Pearl was laying on the couch, on the phone, listening intently to the person that was on the other line. As Reign walked into the living room area, Pearl jumped and hung up on the person who she was on the phone.

"Shit! Reign, you scared the hell out of me!" she said, holding her chest. She looked up at Reign and knew that she had been crying. She said, "What's wrong? Why were you crying?"

"When we had gotten off of the phone earlier, I heard you say something and I need for you to let me know if it was true or not."

"What do you mean? What did I say?" Pearl asked.

"You had said you should have let Senaj fuck you. I need to know what you meant. I already asked him about it and he is denying the whole thing. See, you were the one who said it, you are my best friend so I figured, hey he would lie about it, but I know my best friend wouldn't. Hell, I figured if he did try to fuck you, you would have told me before you felt a certain way about our conversation, that you would have brought it to my attention."

"Sit down, Reign," Peal said. She watched as Reign sat on the couch, on the opposite side of Pearl before she began again, "I wanted to tell you. But you had so much going on that night that I didn't want to add something so minor to it. We had been talking in the car and once we got here, he offered to walk me up to make sure that I was good. So, I didn't think nothing of it. I let him. When we got up here, we got to the door and as I was opening the door, he basically threw himself on me. He said that I was the one that he had been eyeballing from the beginning and that it was me that he wanted. He said that he had only went after you, because he had found out that I was dating somebody and he didn't want to step in between that. I told him that he had to leave, and he had gotten mad. It was so bad, that I had to call for security. I'm sorry, Reign, as your friend I should have been told you. That same night, I should have told you."

Reign had a hard time believing the story. It didn't sound believable. Senaj was aggressive, yes, but that was only in the bedroom. He was a gentleman on the streets. Reign sniffled, as she watched Pearl gather some tears to let them fall from her eyes.

Reign said, "So, you telling me Senaj basically attacked you? That he wasn't checking for me at all and that he basically was using me to get to you?"

"Yes, Reign. And to be quite honest once security came, he had begged me not to tell you."

"So, what was that whole comment that you made, about you should have let him fuck? I mean, you couldn't have been that mad about me holding this grudge against my own uncle, that you felt the need to say that shit about my man. The nigga that I'm fucking," Reign asked, sitting up and placing her elbows on her knees.

Pearl exhaled and said, "Ever since getting pregnant with this baby, I have been acting so bipolar. Saying shit that I don't mean. These hormones and this baby got me fucked up."

Reign looked on at Pearl, as she fidgeted and got up from the couch. She walked inside of the kitchen and poured them a glass of juice and came back. Everything was screaming to Reign that Pearl was lying, but she didn't want to put anything past anyone. She had to find out the truth part of the story.

"Who were you on the phone with? I'm pretty sure that they are waiting for you to call back, being that you had hung up on them," Reign asked, taking a sip from her cup.

"Oh, that was Stanley's mother. She was asking me if I had heard from the police. She had filed a missing person's report on him due to him not contacting her in a few days. I told her that I haven't and that I would be waiting for either the police to call or to wait and see if he would try to contact me. We were ending our conversation when you had walked in."

Reign shook her head and laughed. She laughed until tears fell from her eyes and she sat there looking like a crazy person. Pearl looked on at Reign, wondering what was wrong with her friend.

Reign wiped at her tears and said, "You're lying to me. And I can't seem to figure out why you would feel like you would need to lie to me. I don't know if it's the thing with Senaj or this thing with Stanley's mother, but I definitely think you're lying about something. Pearl, since when we lie to each other, baby girl? We are best friends, that's not what we do."

"Reign, I promise you. I am not lying about anything. I would never do such thing. You the only person that I have in this world and vice versa," Pearl said.

"Pearl, if I find out that you are lying, this friendship is done. I've already dealt with my uncle being a snake. I don't need my best friend turning out to be a snake, too," Reign said, as she got up from the couch and walked to the door.

Everything about the energy in the room was screaming off to Reign. Reign held onto the door knob for a few seconds, trying to gather her thoughts before walking out of the door. She had to do something about everything, but she didn't quite know where to start. Reign swung the door open and walked out of the room.

# Mimi

## Chapter - Sixteen
## Four Months Later

The time for Senaj to walk across the stage had finally came. His graduation was just a few weeks away and he couldn't wait for it to be over. The past four months had been a struggle for him and he constantly heard his brother's words ringing out to him. If only if he would have listened to him in the beginning, then he wouldn't be where he is right now. Sad and heart broken.

In the past four months, he hadn't heard from Reign. After she asked him about Pearl, she dropped from the face of the earth. No phone calls, text messages, emails, nothing. She even had her phone number changed and there had been nothing at her house. Senaj did everything in his power to try to find her, but he came up empty handed. He even went as far as going to Pearl and it wasn't pretty.

*It had been a month since Reign had confronted Senaj at the hospital. Calling her phone and sent text messages went unanswered. He was at his wits end and didn't know what to do. It was hard for him to focus in school, he couldn't eat, or sleep. He often wished that he could go back in time and do things differently. Senaj had gotten tired of not getting a response and he decided to get up and go to Pearl. After all, they were best friends and if Reign didn't believe him, there could still be a possibility that she believed Pearl and would still talk to her.*

*It was late, but not too late where it would have been an inappropriate time to go see Pearl. Senaj walked right through the lobby and onto the elevator. He was on a mission and he refused to have anyone stop him. He rode the elevator up and got off, remembering the stop and the door. He knocked and waited for Pearl to get to the door.*

*"I hope y'all brought exactly what I ordered cause the last two times y'all fucked up!" Pearl said, through the*

*door and then it swung open. Her face registered shock.*

*"I bet I'm the last person that you thought you would see," Senaj said and placed his hands into his pockets.*

*"You damn right! What the fuck are you doing here?" Pearl said, now angered.*

*"You caused my relationship with Reign to end. Have you spoken to her?"*

*"If I have, I wouldn't let you know."*

*Senaj exhaled and said, "Listen I don't have time for your sour ass attitude. It's because of you that she stopped talking to me. I don't know what you said to her, but when I find out it won't be pretty."*

*"I told her the fucking truth!" Pearl yelled.*

*"Please enlighten me about what the fuck the truth was," Senaj said and folded his arms across his chest.*

*"That you tried to fuck me. You pushed yourself on me and you told me that I had been the one you wanted from the beginning."*

*"What?" Senaj roared.*

*"It's been a while since it happened, but I'm pretty sure that you remember. You threw yourself on me and tried to fuck me!"*

*"You really believe that lie you telling? You are nothing compared to Reign. You ain't nothing but a hoe and I'm mad she believed you over me! Fuck you, Pearl! And when she finds out, I hope she do you filthy. I cannot believe that you are so sad with your life that you would want to see your best friend hurt. The same one who is paying for you to stay in this hotel. You have to be some kind of special for you to want to destroy her life." With that Senaj left, leaving more pissed then when he arrived.*

Since that day, he wasn't the same. He had ended up giving up looking for her and tried his hardest to focus on his schooling and work.

Polite and Rasheed had invited him to go out to

celebrate. He was getting ready and he happened to find the dress that she had worn the night they went out for New Year's Eve. He placed it under his nose and sniffed. He missed her so bad, that his heart ached. He put the dress back inside of his closet and decided that if she didn't come back by now that she wouldn't be coming back at all. He was about to become a certified doctor and that needed his focus right now.

Senaj was dressed in some army green jeans, a black graphic tee, and some white high-top Uptowns. He placed his diamond studs in his ears and sprayed on some Seduction by Guess. He headed out to go meet up with his two best friends for a few drinks. They met up at Smalls Jazz Club and it brought old memories back for him. As soon as he got inside, he was requesting for them to go to a different spot.

Slapping fives with Polite and Rasheed, Senaj grabbed his beer and took a seat. The jazz club wasn't crowded at all, since it was only about five in the evening.

They bullshitted around for the first twenty minutes, until Polite decided that he needed to know how his friend was holding up. Since Reign disappeared none of them had said anything about it. They knew better from the last time that she went missing to not pester him about it.

"Senaj, as much as I want to leave it alone, I need to know how you holding up? I know this must be hard for you and I know that you might not want to discuss it-" Polite started to say.

"Then just leave it alone."

"No, man. I wasn't there like that for you the last time and I want to be now. And dammit, females got they friends to vent to and us niggas need to stick together and listen to our friends."

"This isn't the right time to talk about it, Polite. Don't you think? I'm trying to celebrate tonight. I haven't been in a good mood in months and I'm finally enjoying myself," Senaj said, running his hand across his forehead.

Rasheed jumped in and said, "You know what, I think we should get out of here to talk about it. I'm really concerned about you, too."

Senaj raised his eyebrow and looked at them suspiciously. "Since when?"

"Since this the second time this chick done left your ass," Rasheed said.

"Trust me, I'm good this time. There is nothing that I could have done in order for Reign to hear me out. She was dead set on listening to that whore of a friend of hers. I get we weren't together for a long time, but she should have known how I am. I'm only mad at the fact that instead of trusting me, she let that hoe tear us apart."

Rasheed cracked a smile and said, "She is definitely a hoe. I never told y'all but a few days after we met them here, I ran into shorty and she gave them cookies right on up on the hood of my car."

Both Senaj and Polite broke out into laughter.

Senaj said, "Boy, I hope you wrapped that thing up. She out here pregnant. You better hope that ain't your baby. Bitch is certified crazy, and I wouldn't want to wish that on your life."

"I know she pregnant. She found my ass on social media and tried to plant the baby on me, but I did use a condom. She was really drunk, and she thought that I didn't. Pussy was trash, I mean it was hot garbage. Walls was loose, and I think if I didn't hold onto her waist I would have fell inside of her pussy. Trapped forever."

"This nigga here," Polite said, and threw his hands in the air. The whole table erupted in laughter and didn't stop until a waitress came and asked if they wanted another round of beer.

"Actually, no. We're gonna take off," Polite said.

"Y'all finally get me out of the house and y'all only want to spend a half hour here?" Senaj asked.

"I don't know. I'm just not feeling this crowd," Polite said.

"Maybe because it's hella early," Rasheed mentioned.

"So, what do y'all suggest?" Senaj asked.

"Let's just go back to your place and play a few games of Call of Duty and then come back later."

"Man, you childish," Senaj said, causing them to laugh.

They walked out and got inside of their cars and went to Senaj's place. Getting out of the car, they bullshitted for a bit in front of his building before heading up. Polite and Rasheed, while they were excited about their friend's success, they were going to miss the time that they spent with him.

Senaj almost had a heart attack when he opened his door to his apartment and people yelled, "Surprise!"

A smile spread across his face as he searched the crowd. He saw his parents and a few of the people that he knew from the hospital, but his heart was crushed when he didn't see Reign. She was supposed to be around helping him celebrate. He quickly put that feeling to the side and decided to have fun and enjoy himself. His parents were going to spend the next few weeks with him, until it was his day to cross the stage.

\*\*\*

### Three Weeks Later

"Senaj, I can't tell you how much I am proud of you. All of this schooling paid off and can't wait to say that my son is a doctor," Akachi said.

His mother was standing next to his father beaming brightly, with tears in her eyes. They were dressed in typical African attire, as they were in the same colors.

"We are both proud of you," Zain said. She turned to the couch and reached inside of a box that was sitting there. She lifted a sash that was knitted in the same colors that his parents were wearing: green, red, blue, and yellow.

"Maman, what is this for?" Senaj asked his mother.

"This is just something that I would like for you to wear under your gown. It's a gift from your grandparents. They wish you the best and are extremely proud of you as well. They would like for you to take a trip back home soon, and I told them that I would talk you into it," his mother said, with laughter.

Senaj was dressed in black Perry Ellis slacks, with a powder blue Perry Ellis shirt, white tie and black Perry Ellis loafers. He took the sash from his mother and placed it over his shoulder and across his chest. He took his cap from his father and placed it on his head while he draped his gown over his arm.

"Let's take a few pictures before we head out," His father suggested.

For a cool eight minutes they each poised for pictures and then headed on their way. His graduation was being held at the United Palace Theater on Broadway in Manhattan. They arrived in just enough time for his parents to grab seats and for him to get to his. Rasheed and Polite had made it and were in his view. They waved at him, causing Senaj to laugh.

Ten minutes after they arrived, they started the ceremony causing Senaj's gut to rumble with anticipation.

"Congratulations graduates of 2017!" the president of the school, said into the microphone.

Two hours later, they began to call the many students who were graduating. Senaj was in the first round being that his last name began with an "A". His heart was pounding in his chest, and he felt like he was going to have a heart attack. A smile adorned his face, as he walked up the steps to the stage. He was two people away and his hands were sweating.

"Senaj Ademyemi!" His name was being called.

For some reason, he couldn't get his feet to comprehend was his brain was telling them to do. After a few seconds, he laughed at himself and willed his feet to move. He looked into the crowd and saw his parents cheering loudly, along with Rasheed and Polite. He waved as them and continued to walk off the stage as he grabbed his diploma.

*Blacka! Blacka! Blacka!*

Senaj stopped in his steps, as his heart stopped beating in his chest. His first thought was that it was a terrorist attack and he had to get to his parents. As soon as the first shot rang out, there was pandemonium. People were running trying to get out, but it caused people to get trampled on. Fight or flight registered into Senaj's head and he turned to try to get to his parents.

As soon as he did, he ran into what seemed like to be a brick wall. A guy dressed in all black stood in his way. The guy reached his arms in front of him and grabbed Senaj by the throat. Senaj's first instinct was to pop this dude right in the face, and when he did, he broke his own hand on this dude face. He was losing oxygen, as the guy squeezed harder around his neck.

He tried to hit him again, but he was too weak, and his eyes rolled to the back of his head. More shots rang out and luckily for Senaj, the guy who had a boa constrictor like hold on his neck, loosened his grip and fell to his knees. Senaj fell with him as he coughed trying to suck in all of the air that he had missed out on. It was pure chaos, as Senaj got up from the floor. He searched wildly into the crowd for his parents and friends. Someone from behind grabbed him into a choke hold and dragged him towards behind the curtains.

# Mimi

He heard a faint voice as he tried to stay conscious. A voice that he was familiar with. He stopped his eyes from rolling in the back of his head, as he strained to look through the crowd.

"Senaj!" she called out. Her voice was faint, but he could recognize it anywhere. She raised a gun and shot towards him.

"Reign," he whispered, as everything faded to black.

***

*Leaving Senaj is what Reign didn't want to do. Hearing both Pearl and Senaj tell different versions of what happened broke her heart. She never put anything pass anyone and she didn't know who to believe. It was her man against her best friend and while she tried her hardest to believe her man, her loyalty stayed with Pearl. Reign knew that Pearl's story was a little far-fetched, but she also knew that shit happens. She cried for hours after leaving Pearl in the hotel room due to the heartbreak. Her loyalty to Pearl had been questioned, after she sat there and re-evaluated everything that happened. She wrecked her brain to make sense of things but for the life of her she couldn't. Later that night, she meditated deeply. She was searching for answers.*

*The very next day, she left for Sarasota Florida. Her one and only grandmother, her father's mother lived there. Her time to get away was now. She packed up without letting anyone know that she was leaving.*

*As she had gotten off of the airplane at the Sarasota – Bradenton International Airport, she pulled her cell phone from her pocket. She sat on this phone number for months. After not speaking with Senaj the first time, she had gone through a bunch of her old things and found an old journal that she had from sixth grade. She opened it up and read all of the things that she used to write. Laughing at some and then wondering what the hell she was thinking. She came across a page and it had a note on it written to her from her father. It had said that if there was ever anything to happen to him, for her to contact the number that was written below. He had let her know that it was perfectly fine to get in contact with this person. It was her grandmother. And naturally she felt excited being that she never met her. She never thought that she would have to use it. She found herself doing so, as she left out of the airport.*

*She shielded her eyes as she looked at the phone screen and hit dial. She hadn't even been outside for a good ten minutes and she already felt the sweat dripping down the arch in her back and on her top lip. The phone rang for what seemed like forever until an older sounding lady answered the phone.*

*"Hello, Mills' residence," she said.*

*Reign's breath got caught in her throat. This was her first time hearing her grandmother's voice. It was soothing and all she wanted to do was curl up in this woman's lap and tell her all her problems.*

*She sucked it up and said, "Hello. May I speak with Miss Mills, if she's available please?"*

*"Speaking. Who is this?" Miss Mills said, and Reign detected a little sister girl attitude.*

*"I'm sorry to be calling you without a warning at least. I'm your granddaughter," Reign said, and she found herself stumbling over her words.*

*"Hmph! My granddaaughter?"*

*"Yes, ma'am. K.B is my father."*

*"I don't know what kind of games you are trying to pull young lady, but this is not a funny joke. My son has been dead for ten years -"*

*"And I know, Miss Mills. My dad died at my graduation. My mom when I was four. My dad left this number for me, just in case something is to ever happen to him and I just found it. My name is Reign Mills."*

*There was a brief pause, before Reign had to pull the phone away from her ear. Her grandmother scared her and put a smile on her face, all at the same time.*

*Miss Mills was on the other end, "Lawwwwwwd have mercy! This is really my long lost grandbaby! Thank you, Father, for bringing her to me! It's been a long time coming! Praise the Lord!"*

*For a solid minute, Miss Mills spoke in tongues. Reign had to literally scream to get her back to the initial conversation. She said, "Miss Mills-"*

*"No, baby. You can call me grandma or Nana."*

*"Ok, Nana," Reign said, with a smile. She continued, "The reason why I'm calling you is because I was just going through a lot back in New York and I didn't have nowhere to turn to. I know that you barely, no, you don't know me at all-"*

*"Listen here, little girl. There is a reason you came across my number and whether I know you or not, it doesn't matter. How soon can you get to Sarasota?" she said, with a giggle.*

*"What if I told you that I was already here?"*

*"What?" Her grandmother screamed again.*

*Reign repeated herself and her grandmother told her to get her ass back inside of the airport to stay cool and she would be there momentarily. They hung up and Reign did exactly what her grandmother told her to do. All Reign had with her was a Betsey Johnson duffel bag, with a few days' worth of clothes. Her plan was to stay for a few days just to get refreshed.*

*Fifteen minutes later, Reign noticed a tall, curvy, older but glamorous woman walking through the airport. She wore skin tight dark blue denim jeans, a white flowing spaghetti strap shirt, six-inch stiletto sandals, and she was rocking a 26" weave. Reign's mouth fell open, as she walked with so much confidence that Reign couldn't believe that this was her grandmother.*

*"Reign?" Her grandmother spoke.*

*"Nana?" Reign asked. She was truly shocked.*

*"Oh my God! Get up and give me a hug!" Her grandmother yelled.*

*Reign jumped up and gave her grandmother a hug.*

*"It's so good to finally meet you," Reign said.*

*"I wish it would have been sooner. Have you saw your Uncle James yet, since you've been home from the foster care?" she asked, as she tried to grab Reign's bag from her.*

*Reign's ears perked up, cause as sure as hell she ain't never lived in nobodies foster care.*

*"Um, no, ma'am, I haven't been able to get in touch with him," Reign said, trying to hold her composure. She hated that she had to lie, but then there was a method to her madness.*

*Climbing inside of her grandmother's 2017 Ford Fusion, they made small talk on the way to the house. Reign couldn't believe the beautiful scenery, there was several times where she didn't hear a thing her grandmother said.*

*Fifteen minutes later, they pulled up to a 3,000 square foot home that had a circular drive way and the beach as its own playground. Reign stepped out of the car and her mouth dropped, as they got closer and closer to the entrance. There were columns that held up the structure, only indicating that the ceilings on the inside were high. Walking inside, there was a fountain in the middle of the floor and the stair case went up in a slight spiral up to the second level. There were two living rooms downstairs. One of them was all white with silver accents and the other was simple with different shades of brown and was accented with wood.*

*Going to the back of the house on the first level, beyond the fountain was the kitchen and dining room. The dining room had a long cherry oak table with matching chairs and* seated maybe twelve people. There was a crystal chandelier that hung from the ceiling over the table. The kitchen was designed with marble tops, stainless steel appliances and had cherry oak cabinets and drawers, like the dining set in the dining room. Pots and pans hung from a hanging rack over the island, where the glass top stove sat. From the kitchen there was access the beach.

As soon as Reign walked out of the sliding double doors, there was a wooden deck with lounging furniture. The stairs and the sand were the only things that separated Reign from having a good time.

"This is all so dope. Nana, do you live here by yourself?" Reign asked.

"Oh no. I would go crazy and I'm too scary to live in this big ass house alone. Your cousins live with me."

"My cousins?" Reign asked, confused.

"Yeah, James has twins and I believe that they are around your age."

Excitement grew in her heart. She thought she didn't have any family beside James and here it was, she found out she had a grandmother and some cousins.

"Well, where are they? I would love to meet them."

Nana placed a coffee mug on the island and poured herself a cup of steaming coffee. She rolled her eyes and said, "Girl, Jamori and Jackie always on the move. I can't keep up with them. I'd be surprised if they were still in this house."

"Do you have any pictures of them?" Reign asked.

"Of course, I do," Nana said.

She pulled out her Iphone and began searching her pictures. When Reign saw the pictures of her cousins, she not only knew that they belonged to James. Everything about them, was James. Jamori, who was the boy, was tall, maybe six feet three inches and was lean. His teeth were white and bright, he wore his hair in a low ceaser, deep *dimples slim nose and bright almond shaped brown eyes. Jackie, the girl twin, was tall, but not as tall as Jamori. She was maybe five feet eleven inches and she was curvy like their Nana. In the picture, Jackie was rocking a long Brazilian weave and she looked the exact same as Jamori, just girly.*

*"They are cute," Reign said.*

*"They a pain in my ass," Nana said with a chuckle. She continued, "James left them with me when they were just six years old. Their mother had gotten hooked to drugs when they were just six months old. Before James brought me the twins, he told me that her cause of death was due to an overdose. The day that he cremated their mother, was the same day that he brought me the twins. He said he couldn't do it on his own and just left them with me. He used to come often, until they were teenagers and then he stopped all together. He would call them, but they would always wonder why he wouldn't come see them. That was until they just stopped caring."*

*"Has he tried to get in touch with them recently?"*

*"Nope. Whatever he is doing up in New York is way more important than his kids."*

*They talked some more, and Reign briefly brought her Nana up to speed with everything that she had going on with herself, leaving out her love life and what she did to get money. They got along well, and Nana told her stories about her parents that she never knew.*

*Later that evening, the twins came inside of the house and immediately wanted to know who Reign was. When they found out, they were just as excited as she was.*

*For the next four months, she was able to live the life that she wanted to without having to look over her shoulder. She went shopping, spent time on the beach, and went clubbing. Everything was perfect, and Reign actually had the chance to get over the initial hurt that she was feeling about the situation with Senaj and the drama back at home.*

\*\*\*

*Reign had gotten so used to staying in her Nana's house, that she had ultimately started looking for places for her to stay in the area. She was going to move her life all the way to Florida and start over. The second day of her being in Florida, she had changed her number and deactivated any social media accounts that she had. It was approaching the fourth month that she had been down there, and Jackie, Reign, and their Nana was sitting on the deck drinking some wine and enjoying the breeze.*

*"Do you or did you have anyone special back home in New York?" Jackie asked Reign, as she ran her fingers in between her toes.*

*Senaj's face appeared in Reign's memory and she was forced to remember him. She didn't want to, but as she did remember him, a smile spread across her face.*

*Nana saw the smile and said, "By that look I could tell that you did, and I could also tell that you loved him."*

*Exhaling, Reign began, "His name was Senaj. He-"*

*"Ugh, Senaj? What kind of name is that?" Jackie said, turning her nose up.*

*Reign laughed and said, "He's African. He chased me down, until I would take his number. Nana, I didn't just love him, I was, no, I am in love with him. He was the first guy in six years that I dealt with. After dealing with Josiah's cheating ass, I had put this wall up and Senaj was determined to knock it down. And he did so without knowing that he did."*

*"What the hell are you doing here, and he's all the way over there? I know if I'm in love with someone I'm not going to leave their side," Jackie said.*

*"It was complicated."*

*Nana interrupted and said, "Is that the reason why*

*you're down here?"*

*"I'm not going to lie. Partly, yes. After I had found your number, Nana, I wanted to know who the number belonged to. I had gotten sucked into so much stuff that I just didn't have the time. Along with the number that my dad left, there was an address. And my initial thought was to get off the plane and just pop up, but I didn't know how that was going to work out," Reign said, laughing.*

*"I'm glad you did call, cause if you would have showed up here you would have gotten popped. Nana may be old, but I carry heat," Nana said, as she raised her dress up to her thigh where she held a .22 on her thigh.*

*"Nana! You don't want to scare her away!" Jackie yelped.*

*Reign sighed with a smile and got up to walk inside of the house. She could hear Jackie and Nana going back and forth about Reign leaving. She walked into the room that she had been staying in and was only in there for a quick moment. She walked back out on the deck and raised her hands up, causing both Nana and Jackie to stop talking. In her hands were her twin rose gold Maxim 9's.*

*"That's my grand baby!" Nana yelled out causing Reign to smile.*

*"What is wrong with this family! How the hell did you get that down here?" Jackie asked.*

*"I didn't. Remember two months ago when I finally decided to get out of the house? I had my people from up top, bring me some things that I needed. My daddy always told me to make sure I got heat on me. No matter where I go, and I felt naked," Reign explained.*

*"Your daddy taught you right. Now come back and sit your little ass down and let's talk about your boo thing back home."*

*"I really don't want to, Nana. I worked so hard with not thinking about him. It's better that way. If I was to talk*

*about him, my stomach would be all fucked up and I would start missing him again."*

*"Sometimes it's good to talk about things. Maybe it could help you to get over him."*

*"Believe me, Nana. I tried, and it worked until Jackie's ass forced me to remember him," Reign said, with a roll of her eyes.*

*Jackie shot Reign a look and rolled her eyes herself. Reign didn't want to have to go through this. Sure, she missed Senaj at times, but she knew it was time to move on. It was time for her to let it go and get over the heartbreak that she was experiencing. If she ever thought about going back to New York, she wouldn't even entertain the thought of dealing with Senaj again.*

*"Reign, pull up your big girl panties and tell us why you decided to leave a man that you were in love with?" Nana said, growing irritated. She had seen all types of things during her sixty-five years of living and she wasn't a stranger to love. She knew her granddaughter was still in love with this guy, just from the look in her eyes. She wanted to help her realize that she needed to go be with her man, rather than running away from her problems.*

*"He tried to sleep with my best friend," Reign blurted out.*

*Nana raised her eyebrow and asked, "He tried to, or he actually did it?"*

*"According to my best friend, he tried to. I, of course, approached him and asked him what was that all about and he placed the blame on her. Typical nigga shit. I asked her, and she told me that he threw himself on her. That she had said that he wanted her from the beginning but settled for me because he found out that she was with somebody."*

*Both Jackie and Nana looked at Reign, then at each other, and fell back in their chairs in laughter. Reign looked on, like they were crazy.*

# Lipstick Killah

*Nana asked, "Girl, how long you been friends with this girl?"*

*"Since junior high school."*

*"Has your man ever gave you a reason to think that he wanted her?"*

*"No. In fact the night in question, they had officially met for the first time," Reign said.*

*As she spoke, she realized that she was sounding a fool. How could Pearl do her like that? Why would she tell her a lie about Senaj throwing himself in her?*

*"I don't know the girl, but I'm pretty sure that she is lying. If he never gave you the impression, then why would you believe her?" Jackie asked.*

*"Because I never thought that she would lie to me."*

*"It doesn't matter how long you have been friends with a chick, if she's jealous of you for whatever reason, then she will do anything to make sure that you are never happy. Misery loves company, baby girl," Nana said.*

*Then as an afterthought, she continued, "Let me tell you a story. Back before I had decided to have kids, I was friends with this girl. We were as thick as thieves and did everything together. I knew that she didn't have much, because of where she grew up in town. Sad to say, she was from the poor side and my family was on the more wealthier side. I didn't see rich or poor when it came to our friendship. Whatever I had she had. But any who, I digress.*

*"One day, we were hanging out with a few of our other friends and we were playing spin the bottle. It was my turn and as I spun the bottle, it landed on one of the cutest boys that we hung with. I did what I was supposed to do, according to the game rules. I kissed him. A few days passed, and I noticed that I hadn't spoken to her. I went over to her house and when her mother invited me in, I went straight upstairs to her room. Needless to say, she had gotten mad at me because I had kissed him. I told her that*

*it was a part of the game and we went at it for a long while. After that, she didn't talk to me.*

*"Days turned into weeks, weeks turned into months, and I began to miss my friend. The same guy, that I had kissed at the party, approached me and asked me if I would like to go out on a date with him. I didn't think nothing of it, so I went. Word got around that I was seeing him, and her miserable ass started doing little things to piss me off. Back in the day, they were childish as hell. She would put spoiled things inside of my locker, her and her new friends would egg my house, and the last thing that took the cake was when she told my boyfriend that I had a contagious disease. I didn't know what to do and for days I cried. At the time I didn't know that it was her, but I found out months later that it was. Being that I was going through all of this and had no one to turn to, I went back to her so that I could vent, and don't you know that hoe had the nerve to sit there and lie to my face about her doing it. She blamed it on some other girl who had moved just as the school year ended. Said that the girl had a deep hatred for me, being that she was previously dating my boyfriend.*

*"Me being the quite little clever thing that I was back then, I found out where the girl stayed and confronted her. She told me that she had nothing to do with anything that my so-called friend said that she did. In fact, she said that she had been over him way before they even broke up. Needless to say, that I got back home, greased up and went to her side of town and beat her ass. Your Nana didn't and still don't play that. My point is though, love, you can't take word from a jealous bitch. Especially one, that wants what you have."*

*Reign, sitting straight up in her seat said, "Oh shit! What's today?"*

*"May third . why, what's up?" Jackie asked.*

*"Shit! Senaj graduates in a few weeks. I feel like shit."*

# Lipstick Killah

*"What are you going to do about it? You gonna sit here with us lonely heifers or you gonna go get your man?" Nana asked.*

*Jackie threw up her hand and said, "Speak for yourself, Nana. I ain't no lonely heifer. I'm bout to have some dick coming through in a few."*

*Reign's eyes bulged from her head, as she watched Jackie twerk in front of Nana's face. Reign couldn't ever imagine speaking to her grandmother in such manner. She could tell that Nana was used to it, 'cause all she did was get up and start twerking with her. Reign decided that she would go get her man. She was sick without him and she could only imagine how he was feeling without her. She knew one thing for sure, once she saw her man walk across that stage she was going to address the situation and finally get to the bottom of things with Pearl.*

\*\*\*

*Reign arrived early at the United Palace Theater and decided to take a seat all the way in the back, so she wouldn't be noticed. She wanted to surprise Senaj. Reign was afraid that he would just dismiss her, for yet again leaving him. Several times, she thought about him moving on and dealing with someone else. She would be heartbroken and lost. Senaj was her true love and she knew it. At times, she cursed herself for being so dumb and reacting without thinking. Reign made sure that she was looking like a snack, dressed in burgundy high waist slacks, Jimmy Choo sandals, and a white short sleeve shirt. She had gotten thicker in the four months that she was gone, and her hips were popping and her ass juicy. She had done her hair in beach girl's and she wore light natural make-up.*

*The theater started to fill up with graduates and their families and immediately Reign began to look around in hopes of seeing Senaj. She didn't see him anywhere, but her eyes landed on his two best friends. She thought about walking over to say hi and to see if she could get them to tell her how Senaj was holding up, but she decided against it. The ceremony was starting soon and still there was no Senaj. Her heart dropped to her stomach, as she looked around again and that's when she saw him running to his seat. The smile on his face made her heart melt and she couldn't wait for the ceremony to end to approach him.*

*"Senaj Ademyemi!" Applause erupted, and Reign jumped up and acted a fool whooping and hollering. She was proud of him.*

*The sounds of gunshots rang out, causing her to pause momentarily. She reached to the small of her back and quickly scanned the crowd, to see if she saw where the shooting was coming from. People running in different directions made it hard for her to see what was going on. She looked toward the stage where Senaj had been. She saw him damn near fighting for his life, as this giant nigga held him up off the ground by his throat.*

*She took her shoes off and ran in his direction. Tears formed in her eyes. All she wanted to do was save him and it seemed like the closer she got, the further he got. Feeling like she had gotten close enough, she took aim and shot the dude that was holding Senaj by the throat. People were laid out on the ground in front of her, either injured or acting like they were just so that they wouldn't be causality. Reign looked up and saw Senaj getting up and looking through the crowd. He got ready to run and she saw her uncle put Senaj in a choke hold and start dragging him behind the curtains.*

*"Senaj!" Reign screamed. She didn't stop the tears from falling this time.*

*She jumped over the pile of people in front of her and ran towards the stage. She called his name repeatedly, as she watched her uncle drag the love her life. Reign ran with her gun aimed at her uncle and wanted to take a shot, but she feared that she would hit Senaj in the process.*

*Reign saw Senaj shift his eyes to her and looked right at her. She saw a smile on his face, before he mouthed her name. His eyes closed, and she feared the worst. She just knew that she lost him. Reign closed her eyes for a split second and when she opened them, her uncle had his gun aimed at her, with a sinister smile on his face. Within seconds, he vanished behind the curtains and took the man she loved with him.*

# Mimi

## Chapter - Seventeen

It had been two days, since James took Senaj and Reign was going crazy. She had gone back to her house after the ceremony and cried her eyes out. She was mad at herself for leaving him. She thought of all the places that her uncle could have taken him and put a plan together. She hadn't had any sleep, because she was preparing for a war. She could only imagine what his parents and friends were feeling. She was walking around her house getting her things ready when she received a phone call from her grandmother.

"Hey, Nana," she said, sniffling.

"What's wrong? Why have you been crying child?" Nana asked.

"Nana! Everything is all wrong!" she cried. She was damn near hyperventilating.

"Girl, hush up all that crying. Catch your breath and tell me what the fuck is going on."

Reign took a few moments to catch her breath and began to explain what was going on. She said, "Nana, I'm sorry I lied to you. After Daddy died Uncle James took me in as his own and was watching over me. I took over the business where Daddy left off. I can't say too much over the phone, but for the past few months Uncle James and I had been beefing. He has been trying to set me up for some money Daddy left that I knew nothing about. I came home for Senaj's ceremony, as you know, and chaos happened. He came up in the theater and turned shit up and kidnapped him!" Reign screamed.

Nana exhaled and said, "Listen to me and listen to me good. I accept your apology, because I knew you were lying. I kept tabs on you, girl, and only hoped that you would hurry up and use that information that your father left. I know what K.B was into. Where you think he got it from?

Your whole family is all the same and when I get the chance to tell you I will, but you need to hear me and hear me good. I just got off the plane with Jamori and Jackie, because I knew this was going to happen. I'm waiting for Jamori to rent this car and I'm coming straight to you. Your uncle is not related by blood. It was your cousin's mother, who was my daughter and I knew for years that your uncle was scheming. He is getting what's coming to him and I won't let you fight this fight without me. Do you understand me?"

"Yes, but, Nana…"

"Nana, my ass. Do as I say and just wait for us."

"Okay, Nana." With that they hung up the phone and Reign was in disbelief.

She sat on the floor in her living room and couldn't help but to laugh like a mad woman. The whole time, she thought she was doing some shit by covering herself up, her grandmother already knew everything. She wondered if her cousins knew or if they were just riding along with their grandmother. Reign took her phone from her pocket to text her cousin Jackie, but she noticed that Jackie had already texted her. It read:

*Jackie: We knew everything from the beginning. My dad is going to get what is coming to him. Nana had been training Jamori and I since we were thirteen. She told us the truth about him being the cause of our mother passing. He knew she was a drug addict and instead of helping her, he stuck a needle full of rat poison into her veins. Don't worry, Cuz, we got your back.*

Reign's laughter, if she was in a room full of people would have been described as something like a psychotic patient. Feeling better already and having faith that her baby would be found, she made her way to her kitchen, where there was a door that led to her basement.

She walked down the stairs and walked into her own private armory. There were guns all over the place and she never felt more alive. Reign moved about the basement, loading up duffel bag after duffel bag of guns.

She had been down in the basement for ten minutes, when she heard her bell ringing. She grew excited and ran up the basement stairs, leaving the door open anticipating her family. She swung the door open and was met with a punch straight to her chest. It knocked the wind out of her and she slid down the hall landing in a heap at the bottom of her stairs. She struggled to get her breathing in order, as she struggled to get up. The talk dark figure moved towards her at the speed of light and tried to grab her, but she grab his leg and twisted it, causing him to fall.

Reign jumped up and leaned against the nearest wall. The guy yelled in agony, but still got up and went after her. Using all her strength, Reign delivered two haymakers to the face and hit him in the stomach. She thought that would slow him down, but he just kept on. He threw a left hook which missed her by inches, but he quickly recovered that hit and delivered an uppercut so powerful, that it caused her to lift up in the air as if she was in a cartoon and dropped her like a bag of laundry. It dazed her momentarily.

He walked over to her, grabbed her up by the neck and lifted her in the air. Losing oxygen and knowing that she couldn't go out like that, she delivered a kick swiftly to the nuts. He screamed out like a little girl as he dropped to his knees. Reign was leaking blood from her mouth and nose. Grabbing the lamp that she had in the corner of the room, she picked it up and smashed it over his head.

"Who the fuck are you?" Do you not know who you fucking with?" she yelled, spitting blood onto the back of his head.

Leaning on one knee, the guy stood up and she got a good look at his face. While she didn't know who he was, he looked familiar. He screamed and ran in her direction and she hauled ass.

# Mimi

*'Is he some kind of super fucking human? Why won't he quit?'* she thought to herself.

Reign stopped in her footsteps, causing him to halt in his and as he stood there stunned and wondering why she had stopped abruptly. She jumped up and roundhouse kicked him, lifting his body from the ground. Before touching the ground again, his body effortlessly twisted twice in a circle and this time he was the one who fell like a bag of laundry.

Taunting him, Reign said, "You must have thought that this was going to be a walk in the park! Coming in here and putting your hands on a female. You got the right one! I ain't down without a fight!"

*Smacccccccccccck!*

Reign felt like a mac truck had hit her. For sure, she thought that her jaw was hanging from her face only by the muscle. Reign had been smacked before and it only caused her to feel a little stinging. He smacked her so hard, she was literally seeing stars. She laid on the floor and he stood over her, laughing the same laugh, that she was just laughing.

She had to admit to herself that she had never fought with someone who was equally as good as herself. As she felt this hulk-like guy dragging her to the kitchen, she saw Senaj's face flash in her memory. She had to fight this guy to get to her baby and now would not be a good time for her to give up. She twisted and turned, as she tried to get loose.

Entering into the bright kitchen, she ran her hand under the fridge quickly, as he dragged her by the hair, where she knew there was a blade that was under it. She remembered that she had dropped it and never went back to pick it up. With all the little bit of energy that she had left, she sliced at his hand. She didn't stop until after he finally felt it and let her go.

Her face was now covered in blood, his mixed with hers. Her face was swollen, and her body ached. She knew that this was it. She was accepting the fact that she was about to go on to the upper room. This guy seemed like he was like the energizer bunny and he was going to keep on going and going.

*"I always heard that I will meet my match, I never thought it would be the hulk.'* Reign thought to herself.

Seeing that she had no more fight in her left, The Hulk leaned down and looked at her. Her hair was covering her face and he used his good hand to remove the hair from her face. Reign tried her hardest to focus on him, as her eyes rolled to the back of her head. Tears escaped as she prayed to God that he would watch over Senaj and to help find it in her uncle's heart to let Senaj go.

"If you are going to kill me, do it now. I don't have any more fight in me left," Reign said.

In one swift movement, he wrapped his hand around her neck and squeezed. There was no fight from her. He leaned next to her ear, just as she was inches away from losing oxygen.

He whispered in her ear, "Where is my brother?"

She couldn't believe it. Her eyes bulged, and she began grabbing at his hands, to try to get them off. She managed to say, "A—Akuchi—ppppplease. I'm pregnant with his baby."

*To Be Continued...*
Lipstick Killah 2
Coming Soon

**<u>Coming Soon from Lock Down Publications/Ca$h</u>**
**<u>Presents</u>**

BOW DOWN TO MY GANGSTA

By **Ca$h**

TORN BETWEEN TWO

By **Coffee**

BLOOD STAINS OF A SHOTTA **II**

By **Jamaica**

WHEN THE STREETS CLAP BACK **II**

By **Jibril Williams**

STEADY MOBBIN

By **Marcellus Allen**

BLOOD OF A BOSS **V**

By **Askari**

BRIDE OF A HUSTLA **III**

By **Destiny Skai**

WHEN A GOOD GIRL GOES BAD **II**

By **Adrienne**

LOVE & CHASIN' PAPER **II**

By **Qay Crockett**

THE HEART OF A GANGSTA **III**

By **Jerry Jackson**

LOYAL TO THE GAME **IV**

By **T.J. & Jelissa**

A DOPEBOY'S PRAYER **II**

By **Eddie "Wolf" Lee**

# Lipstick Killah

IF LOVING YOU IS WRONG… **III**

By **Jelissa**

BLOODY COMMAS **III**

SKI MASK CARTEL

By **T.J. Edwards**

BLAST FOR ME **II**

By **Ghost**

A DISTINGUISHED THUG STOLE MY HEART **III**

By **Meesha**

ADDICTIED TO THE DRAMA **II**

By **Jamila Mathis**

LIPSTICK KILLAH **II**

By **Mimi**

<u>**Available Now**</u>

**(CLICK TO PURCHASE)**

<u>RESTRAINING ORDER</u> **I & II**

By **CA$H & Coffee**

<u>LOVE KNOWS NO BOUNDARIES</u> **I II & III**

By **Coffee**

<u>RAISED AS A GOON</u> I, II & III

By **Ghost**

<u>LAY IT DOWN</u> **I & II**

<u>LAST OF A DYING BREED</u>

By **Jamaica**

<u>LOYAL TO THE GAME</u>

<u>LOYAL TO THE GAME II</u>

<u>LOYAL TO THE GAME III</u>

# Mimi

By **TJ & Jelissa**

BLOODY COMMAS I & II

By **T.J. Edwards**

IF LOVING HIM IS WRONG…I & II

By **Jelissa**

WHEN THE STREETS CLAP BACK

By **Jibril Williams**

A DISTINGUISHED THUG STOLE MY HEART I & II

By **Meesha**

PUSH IT TO THE LIMIT

By **Bre' Hayes**

BLOOD OF A BOSS **I, II, III & IV**

By **Askari**

THE STREETS BLEED MURDER **I, II & III**

THE HEART OF A GANGSTA I & II

By **Jerry Jackson**

CUM FOR ME

CUM FOR ME 2

CUM FOR ME 3

An **LDP Erotica Collaboration**

BRIDE OF A HUSTLA **I & II**

THE FETTI GIRLS **I, II& III**

By **Destiny Skai**

WHEN A GOOD GIRL GOES BAD

By **Adrienne**

A GANGSTER'S REVENGE **I II III & IV**

THE BOSS MAN'S DAUGHTERS

THE BOSS MAN'S DAUGHTERS II

192

## Lipstick Killah

A SAVAGE LOVE **I & II**

BAE BELONGS TO ME

A HUSTLER'S DECEIT I, II

By **Aryanna**

A KINGPIN'S AMBITON

A KINGPIN'S AMBITION **II**

I MURDER FOR THE DOUGH

By **Ambitious**

TRUE SAVAGE

TRUE SAVAGE II

TRUE SAVAGE **III**

By **Chris Green**

A DOPEBOY'S PRAYER

By **Eddie "Wolf" Lee**

WHAT ABOUT US **I & II**

NEVER LOVE AGAIN

THUG ADDICTION

By **Kim Kaye**

THE KING CARTEL **I, II & III**

By **Frank Gresham**

THESE NIGGAS AIN'T LOYAL **I, II & III**

By **Nikki Tee**

GANGSTA SHYT **I II &III**

By **CATO**

THE ULTIMATE BETRAYAL

By **Phoenix**

BOSS'N UP **I , II & III**

By **Royal Nicole**

# Mimi

<u>I LOVE YOU TO DEATH</u>
**By Destiny J**
<u>I RIDE FOR MY HITTA</u>
<u>I STILL RIDE FOR MY HITTA</u>
By **Misty Holt**
<u>LOVE & CHASIN' PAPER</u>
By **Qay Crockett**
<u>TO DIE IN VAIN</u>
By **ASAD**
<u>BROOKLYN HUSTLAZ</u>
By **Boogsy Morina**
<u>BROOKLYN ON LOCK I & II</u>
By **Sonovia**
<u>GANGSTA CITY</u>
By **Teddy Duke**

Lipstick Killah

**BOOKS BY LDP'S CEO, CA$H**

**(CLICK TO PURCHASE)**

TRUST IN NO MAN

TRUST IN NO MAN 2

TRUST IN NO MAN 3

BONDED BY BLOOD

SHORTY GOT A THUG

THUGS CRY

THUGS CRY 2

THUGS CRY 3

TRUST NO BITCH

TRUST NO BITCH 2

TRUST NO BITCH 3

TIL MY CASKET DROPS

RESTRAINING ORDER

RESTRAINING ORDER 2

IN LOVE WITH A CONVICT

**Coming Soon**

BONDED BY BLOOD 2

BOW DOWN TO MY GANGSTA